"I could ... **_Michael said._**

It hadn't been a question, but she answered anyway. "Yes."

His fingers caressed her satiny cheek while his thumb pressed against her lips. "You want me as much as I want you. Why don't you admit you'd like to stay with me tonight?"

"I would like to stay."

His eyes blazed in triumph, and he began to pull her to him.

"But I'm not going to."

Instead of demanding to know why, he accepted her refusal. Smiling at her, he said, "It's enough to know you want to . . . for now."

"You still want to see me after . . . I mean, I didn't . . . ?"

He chuckled. "Did you expect me to pout when you said no?"

She looked shy. "Maybe sulk a little. Some men do."

He lowered his head and brushed her lips with his. "When are you going to realize I'm not like most men?"

She ran her tongue over her lips, savoring the taste of him. "I think I already know that."

"Good Lord, Diana, don't do that to me. Do you have any idea what it's like, watching your tongue stroking your flesh? Someday, moon goddess, I'm going to feel it on mine. . . ."

WHAT ARE *LOVESWEPT* ROMANCES?

They are stories of true romance and touching emotion. We believe those two very important ingredients are constants in our highly sensual and very believable stories in the *LOVESWEPT* line. Our goal is to give you, the reader, stories of consistently high quality that may sometimes make you laugh, sometimes make you cry, but are always fresh and creative and contain many delightful surprises within their pages.

Most romance fans read an enormous number of books. Those they truly love, they keep. Others may be traded with friends and soon forgotten. We hope that each *LOVESWEPT* romance will be a treasure—a "keeper." We will always try to publish

LOVE STORIES YOU'LL NEVER FORGET
BY AUTHORS YOU'LL ALWAYS REMEMBER

The Editors

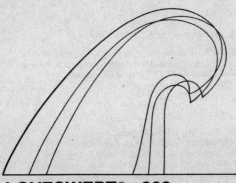

LOVESWEPT® • 202

Patt Bucheister
Touch the Stars

BANTAM BOOKS
TORONTO • NEW YORK • LONDON • SYDNEY • AUCKLAND

TOUCH THE STARS

A Bantam Book / August 1987

If you would be interested in receiving protective vinyl covers for your Loveswept books, please write to this address for information:

Loveswept
Bantam Books
P.O. Box 985
Hicksville, NY 11802

ISBN 0-553-21815-8

Published simultaneously in the United States and Canada

Bantam Books are published by Bantam Books, Inc. Its trademark, consisting of the words "Bantam Books" and the portrayal of a rooster, is Registered in U.S. Patent and Trademark Office and in other countries. Marca Registrada. Bantam Books, Inc., 666 Fifth Avenue, New York, New York 10103.

PRINTED IN THE UNITED STATES OF AMERICA

O   0 9 8 7 6 5 4 3 2 1

To Elaine,

who first introduced me to the joys of
the written word.
My friend, my biggest fan, my mother.

One

Flashbulbs from several cameras nearly blinded Diana as she came out of the courtroom. Microphones connected to tape recorders were shoved in her face as questions were fired at her one after the other, even on top of one another, like bullets from a machine gun.

She felt a suffocating panic as memories assaulted her of another time, eight years earlier, when hordes of reporters had flocked around her and her family like hungry vultures. This time the newspaper and television newshounds weren't digging for juicy, scandalous headlines, but they were as insistent and relentless as ever.

Diana Dragas was a heroine, a bona fide, Grade A heroine, a woman who had bravely faced danger when she'd saved a man's life . . .

With her shoe.

Somehow the young defendant had managed to smuggle a gun into the courtroom, and had aimed it at Judge Dare. Diana's first thought had been to get the gun away from the desperate sixteen-year-old boy before he could carry out the threat to the judge's life. The boy was in enough trouble. She had wanted to stop him from getting into more. Of course, if he pulled the trigger, he wouldn't do the judge much good either. She had been too far away to grab the gun, so she had simply yanked off one of her shoes and thrown it at the boy's hand. It had been a spontaneous act, and pure luck that she had actually managed to knock the gun out of his hand before he pulled the trigger.

The brave public defender had slithered out from under the table, where he had hidden as soon as the gun appeared, and managed to pick it up off the floor while the bailiffs surrounded the boy and led him away. The boy left without looking at her. Since she was the last person the teenager had wanted to see just then, her services were no longer needed in the courtroom.

Judge Dare had taken the time to thank her for her quick action, and other people had swarmed around her before she had been able to leave the courtroom. Unfortunately, the delay had given the media time to gather like piranhas finding fresh meat.

Now she had to make her way through the news people who had come out of the woodwork—which was where she would consign them if she had a choice. It must have been a slow day in San Francisco, she thought, if she was the best thing the reporters could find at the moment.

The questions came thick and fast.

"Did you break his wrist?"

"Have you ever done this kind of thing before?"

"What kind of gun was it?"

That last idiotic question made Diana give the woman journalist a look of scorn, but it didn't faze the intrepid reporter. She came back with, "What size shoe do you wear?"

A photographer caught Diana's mouth dropping open in astonishment at the stupidity of the question.

She was about to give the woman a blistering retort, when a distinctive male voice penetrated the rabble of questions. A strong hand closed around hers and plucked her out of the crowd. "This way, lady."

Somehow the hand managed to maneuver her out of the midst of cameras and people, and she was pulled into a room off the wide corridor. She had a blurred impression of a tall man with brown hair as she was whisked by an open door with a brass plate stuck on it at eye level. She managed to read the nameplate before she was hauled inside, and she grinned at the unusual choice of sanctuary. If this guy was a reporter, he showed a fair amount of imagination. His hand gripped her shoulders, forcing her to stand still. "Stay there," he ordered.

She felt like a horse that had been encouraged to race at full gallop, only to have its reins yanked.

While she watched, he pulled a table over to block the door, giving her a view of his slim hips in tight jeans, and his broad shoulders encased in a navy corduroy jacket worn over a white shirt. When he turned around, giving her a clear view of his face, she guessed he was in his mid-thirties. His skin was tanned, indicating he spent time outdoors, and she was close enough to see laugh lines radiating from the corners of his dark, sable eyes. He gave an impression of strength, and not just a physical strength. She sensed in him the self-confidence of a man who knew who he was and was comfortable with the knowledge. There was no sign of a tape recorder, camera, or notebook.

He levered himself onto the tabletop, sitting nonchalantly with his hands resting on either side of his thighs. The door clunked against the table as someone tried to shove it open from the other side, but he obstinately stayed where he was.

His amused brown eyes met hers. "You might want to join me up here. You don't look like you weigh much, but every little bit would help."

For a long moment Diana looked at him. Then, with a shrug, she walked over to the table. She boosted herself up and sat next to him, her shoeless feet dangling off the floor. "You aren't one of them, are you?" she asked.

He looked at her with curiosity. She made "them" sound like something slimy found under a rock, he thought. "A newspaper reporter? No." He held out his right hand toward her. "I'm Michael Dare."

She put her hand in his. After a slight hesitation, she gave her name. "Diana Dragas."

His gaze went from her smile to her eyes, their unusual color stunning him for a moment. He didn't realize he still held her hand until she tugged to be released, bringing him back out of the turquoise pool he had fallen into. A man could drown in those eyes, he mused.

"You have the most incredible eyes I've ever seen, Diana Dragas," he murmured huskily.

Diana swung her legs casually under the table. "I never know quite how to answer when people say that. I feel awkward saying thank you, since I can't very well take the credit for the color of my eyes. If I say I know, people think I'm conceited. If I ignore it, I'm rude." She paused a moment. "Did you say your name was Dare?"

He nodded absently, still mesmerized by her eyes and conversation. Her voice sounded like whiskey-soaked velvet. She spoke with a slight English accent, which made him wonder about her background. "Michael Dare," he repeated.

He waited for the usual comment about how she had seen him many times on various programs, but she didn't show any sign of recognition at all, just curiosity.

"Any relation to Judge Nathaniel Dare?" she asked.

The door bumped against the table again, jolting them slightly. They both ignored it.

"He's my uncle," Michael said. "I thought the least I could do for the woman who saved my uncle's life was to rescue her from the cameras. That's some aim you have, by the way. Why did you throw a shoe?"

"It was the only thing I could think of. My purse was on one of the benches. So you were in the courtroom?"

He nodded. "When we had lunch, my uncle sug-

gested I sit in on one of his sessions in juvenile court."
He smiled down at her. "I was expecting a dry, boring
case involving some minor offense, like shoplifting or
breaking a window. Instead I see shoes flying through
the air."

"One shoe."

He smiled at her crisp correction. "One shoe." There
were still sounds of activity on the other side of the
door. "We're going to have to wait here until the security men get rid of the reporters."

"We may have a long wait."

Someone was now pounding on the door rather
strongly. He gave her a crooked smile. "They don't give
up, do they?"

She smiled back, a glint of amusement in her eyes.
"It could be a desperate woman in need of the facilities."

"What facilities?"

"These facilities. In case you haven't noticed, this is
the ladies' rest room."

Michael glanced around, taking in the stalls, sinks,
and mirrors for the first time. Turning back to her, he
grinned. "I'll be darned. So it is." His gaze roamed
around the room again, a curious frown creasing his
brow. "I'm disappointed."

"What did you expect?"

"I don't know, exactly, but this isn't it. I have to
admit I haven't really given ladies' rest rooms a great
deal of thought, but I suppose I expected them to be a
bit more feminine."

Diana laughed, enjoying the ridiculous conversation.
"Did you expect lace curtains, fresh flowers, and crystal decanters?"

"No, but something not quite so sterile." A corner of
his mouth twisted into a teasing smile. "Is it true there
are all sorts of naughty sayings on the backs of the
doors?"

She flung her hand toward the stalls. "Be my guest."

After a short pause, he shook his head. "No. Some things are better left to the imagination." His eyes glittered with a roguish light. "What's a nice girl like you doing in a place like this?"

"Some strange guy dragged me in here."

"I object," he said, sounding wounded but looking amused. "I am not strange. I was being gallant, saving you from that pack of reporters. You didn't look like you were enjoying the experience."

"That's an understatement."

He heard the bitterness in her voice. "Camera-shy, are we?"

"Something like that." She stuck one of her stock-inged feet out for his inspection. "Look at this. A re-porter took the shoe I threw, probably to take a photo of it, and never gave it back. I had to take the other one off so I could walk. One of them even asked what size shoe I wear."

"I heard. Not one of the brightest questions ever asked."

She made a scoffing sound. "It was asinine and stu-pid," she said, then added bitingly, "and typical."

He raised a brow in surprise. "Apparently you don't care for the world of journalism, or is it just stupid questions you don't like?"

"The one comes with the other," she said nastily, sliding off the table.

Watching her as she walked to a sink and began washing her hands, Michael considered her opinion of journalists in general. She certainly had a way with words, direct and to the point. It was obvious she didn't like journalists in any form. That rather put an end to an in-depth discussion about his work—not that she had the faintest idea what he did . . . or that she cared. To her, he was Judge Dare's nephew, pe-riod. The fact that she didn't know who he was irked him. Didn't she ever watch television, for Pete's sake? Even though he was no longer a network newscaster, his documentaries were on the air several times a year. His most recent one, on homeless street people, was up for an award, and he had appeared throughout the film. Apparently she had missed it.

Her reaction wasn't what he usually received from women. Perhaps he had been spoiled. He knew women liked to be seen with him, enjoyed the high-powered people he associated with, the exciting field he worked in. He was also fully aware of his own attractiveness. For some strange reason women were drawn by his cavalier attitude toward them. He could take them or leave them, and usually he did both.

He studied her profile. Then a corner of his mouth curved upward as his gaze roamed over the luscious curves of her slender body. His decision to help her get away from the crowd of reporters had been strictly impulsive. There had been no ulterior motive, no selfish attempt to score points with a beautiful woman. Because of her, his uncle would continue to live a fairly healthy life, cussing his golf score and smoking those horrible cigars he liked.

Gratitude might have motivated him to spring into action, but there was something about her that crowded out benign gratitude. There was nothing benign about the way his body was reacting to the sight of the soft swell of her hips and her thrusting breasts. What was it about her that was disturbing him? She was not a classical beauty, but she had a presence, a magnetic pull on his senses he was finding difficult to resist.

When his gaze came back to her face, she was staring directly at him.

Diana recognized the look in his eyes, accepting his curiosity and interest without embarrassment or vanity. She would have enjoyed the luxury of studying him, too, but this was neither the time nor the place. Somehow a ladies' rest room had never struck her as a great setting for striking up an acquaintance with a man. Her first priority was to get out of the courthouse without the reporters having a go at her again.

Michael managed to bring his wandering thoughts back to a more innocent subject. "Most women would have screamed bloody murder the minute they saw a gun," he said.

She gave him a wry glance. "I thought the public defender did enough screaming before he dove under the table. It wouldn't have done any good to scream anyway. The boy is deaf."

She lifted her hands and began to remove the pins holding her abundant hair in a complicated twist behind her head. A wavy, shiny black curtain of hair fell onto her shoulders and down her back. She didn't hear the sharp intake of breath from the man seated on the table. Bending over at the waist, she ran her fingers through her hair several times to loosen the strands, fluffing the hair into a mussed veil of black. Straightening up, she tossed her head back, and the mass of hair settled into a completely different style around her face.

Michael felt his heart thud in his chest at the provocative sight in front of him. This was how she would look after making love, he thought. Heat pulsed through his lower body. He wanted to see that tousled hair spread over a pillow, to run his fingers through it as he covered her body with his.

Good Lord, he had better stop thinking along those lines or he wouldn't be able to get off the table without its being obvious where his thoughts had wandered off to.

Deciding to stick to general conversation, he asked, "How did you know the boy is deaf?"

"That's why I was in the courtroom."

She was giving him answers that weren't really answers. "Would you explain that?"

"I was supposed to interpret the questions and answers for him in sign language," she said as she removed the white silk tie that had been arranged in a loose bow down the front of her blouse and stuffed it into her purse. Then she turned up her shirt collar and unfastened several buttons. "That's part of my job," she continued. "I'm an interpreter. And in answer to your next question, yes, it is an unusual occupation, but I enjoy it."

She slipped off her black suit jacket, pulled the sleeves inside out to expose the red silk lining, then slid the reversed jacket back on. She now wore a bright red jacket with her black skirt.

Michael tried again to grasp sanity. "Is there much demand for an interpreter of sign language?"

"No, not a lot, but I also speak and write in five languages. Six, counting English. Seven, counting American English, which differs considerably from the Queen's English."

Michael let that bit of information soak in. There was no boasting in her statement, just the bald facts that made him more curious about her than ever. And concentrating on her job was better for his libido than wondering what she was going to take off next.

Clearing his throat, he asked, "And there is a demand for someone who speaks so many languages?"

She smiled at the bewilderment in his voice. People usually found her occupation a bit odd. "San Francisco draws a wealth of people from different cultures. Not all of them speak or write English. That's where I come in, or someone like me. I work out of an agency that specializes in supplying people for unusual jobs."

Michael tamped down his impatience, unsatisfied with the vague information she was doling out. "So you teach English?" he asked, taking a stab in the dark.

"Among other things."

"Like what?"

She tilted her head to one side. "You ask a lot of questions, for someone who says he isn't a reporter."

He saw the wariness in her eyes and sought to dispel it. "I'm incredibly snoopy."

She agreed with him. "Yes, you are."

She withdrew from her purse a plastic package containing a pair of folded leather slippers. In a few seconds they were on her feet.

"Do you usually carry slippers around with you?" he asked.

"I bought these earlier today." Her eyes met his, and she smiled slowly when she saw the slightly bemused look on his face. "Well, what do you think? Do I look different?"

He nodded. "Definitely different." The business lady was gone. A provocative woman had taken her place. "I assume this interesting transformation is for the benefit of any reporters hanging around outside."

"They will be looking for a woman dressed in a business suit, with her hair up and without any shoes. They look at the surface, at the obvious."

His smile held a hint of admiration. "I should warn you. If there are any male reporters out there, they will still want to question you, but the questions will be of a more personal nature. Like asking if you're free for dinner."

Her laughter acknowledged the compliment but showed she didn't take it seriously. As she walked toward him, he slowly slid off the table, and was standing when she stopped in front of him.

"I want to thank you for rescuing me." Her gaze shifted briefly around the room. "Your methods may be a bit unorthodox, but they work."

Lord, he wanted to touch her. "Why do I get the feeling you're saying good-bye?"

"Probably because I am."

It was no use. He had to touch her. He raised his hand. The back of his fingers touched the side of her face. Satin. Warm, tantalizing satin.

"Not yet," he said. He lifted a lock of hair off her shoulder, and his gaze rested on the soft strand of black silk curling around his finger as if it were trying to chain him to her.

"Who are you, Diana?" he asked softly.

Startled more by his touch and tone of voice than by the question, she said, "The last part of that question answered the first part. I'm Diana."

"That's your name. I want to know about you. I want to know how you learned to speak so many languages. I want to know where you live. Why you don't like reporters." He tugged at the curl forcing her to look up at him. His voice lowered. "Why I don't want to let you out of my sight yet."

Her dark lashes lowered, cutting off the brilliance of her astonishing eyes. "You want a lot."

"You'd be surprised at how much I want."

She met his gaze unflinchingly, recognizing the gleam of interest in his dark eyes. "You move right along, don't you?"

"Sometimes."

"How about if you *move* that table out of the way and we *move* out of here?"

"On one condition." He released her hair. "Have a drink with me."

"Why?"

"Because I'm thirsty. Because a restaurant is a better place to talk than a ladies' powder room. Because it's a good excuse to spend more time with you."

She considered the invitation, and was surprised that she was considering it at all. "Sorry. I have a ferry to catch."

He blinked. "You catch fairies?" Oddly enough, it wouldn't surprise him that she would try.

It was Diana's turn to be puzzled. A little hesitantly, she replied, "Only one. The Golden Gate Ferry. I live in Sausalito."

Recovering quickly, he said, "I'll drive you home."

She shook her head. "No, thanks."

They looked at each other for a long moment, then moved apart. She helped him drag the table away from the door. The security guards had done their job. The corridor was clear of news people.

"It looks like you went through your transformation for nothing," Michael said as they left the ladies' rest room. "The reporters have vanished."

"You don't know them like I do."

He could have debated that point with her, but didn't.

When a few women looked startled to see a man coming out of what they considered their private territory, Diana choked back a laugh. When she glanced up at Michael, the bland expression on his face told her he had seen them, too, and was amused by their reaction.

There were several reporters waiting outside, even though it was raining. Diana slanted a smug look at Michael. He grimaced in return. She had been right. The reporters had hung around. Their gazes swept over and past Diana when she didn't meet the requirements of the woman they were waiting for. They didn't look at all happy as they clustered under umbrellas, watching for their prey to come out of the building.

"You were right," Michael murmured. "They're looking for the woman you left back in the ladies' room."

"The only imagination reporters have comes out when they write an article. Then they come up with some real great stories, pure fiction. What they can't find in the way of news, they fill in with suppositions."

There was that distaste for news people again, he thought, and looked up at the gray sky and the rain. "Do you happen to have an umbrella tucked away in that purse?" he asked.

She shook her head. "That's one thing I don't have."

"Then let me give you a ride to the Ferry Building."

She gazed up at him for a moment, then at the rainy skies, then back at him. Making a sudden decision against her better judgment, she agreed. "All right."

Before she changed her mind, he started down the steps, saying over his shoulder, "Wait here. I'll go get my car."

"A little rain won't hurt me," she said as she followed, catching up to him after only a few steps.

His hand closed around her arm as they walked quickly across the rain-slick street.

In a day full of surprises, Diana had another one waiting for her when Michael stopped next to a red car.

She stared. "Is this yours?" she asked in astonishment.

He dug his car keys out of his pocket and unlocked the passenger door. "Every nut and bolt."

Her eyes skimmed over the lines of the rare car. "What year is it?"

"It's a 1957 Thunderbird," he said, then added, "Could we discuss the car from the inside? I think my shoes are shrinking."

The upholstery was a rich red leather, and Diana wondered if it was the original covering. Her glance shifted to the man striding around the front of the car, and she noticed he wasn't particularly hurrying to get out of the pouring rain, even though he had complained about getting wet. Blast the man, she thought. Why did he have to be charming, funny, and own a classic car? She had a penchant for the unusual, the offbeat, much to the dismay of her proper English mother, and he was beginning to fit that category in her mind. Marching to a different drummer had been her stride for a long time, and few people she knew could keep up with her. This man just might be the exception.

Leaning over to the driver's side, she unlocked the door. Then he was beside her in the close confines of the car.

Raindrops lingered on his dark hair. He ran a hand over his wet face, and glanced over at her. His expression was puzzled, his eyes curious, as he asked, "Why are you looking at me like that?"

She felt her cheeks grow warm, and she copied his gesture of wiping the rain off her skin, hoping he didn't notice her heightened color. She didn't believe it. She was actually blushing like a teenager caught gawking at the new gorgeous science teacher. She never blushed.

Her pride brought her eyes to his. "How am I looking at you?"

"Like you've just stepped into a lion's den and you're wondering how big the lion's teeth are. You can relax. I don't bite."

She pulled her clinging, damp blouse away from her body, unaware that her action drew his gaze to her feminine curves. "I'm not afraid of you. Surprised, maybe, and a bit curious about why a man like you would drive a classic car, but I'm definitely not afraid of you."

He shifted in his seat to face her, his arm resting along the top of the seat. "What kind of car would you expect a man like me to drive?"

Shrugging, Diana wished she had kept her thoughts to herself. "A Corvette, a Ferrari, a Jaguar. Something sleek, fast, and expensive."

His eyes narrowed as he considered her answer. "Do you prefer sleek, fast, expensive men?"

"Not particularly," she replied vaguely. "Could we get going? I don't want to miss the next ferry."

"You started this. You've made a snap judgment about the type of man I am without knowing anything about me. According to my uncle, His Honor the judge, a man has a right to self-defense. I suggest you hold off your verdict until you get to know me better."

"You're expecting a lot out of a short ride to the ferry landing, aren't you?" she asked with amusement.

He started the engine. "Horse races are run in about

a minute and a half. It takes three minutes to boil an egg. Some things don't take a lot of time."

She laughed. "Confident devil, aren't you?" She looked out at the rain bouncing off the glass in front of her. "Does this antique have windscreen wipers?"

"Of course."

"Don't you think it would be a good idea to turn them on? It happens to be raining."

"Where's your spirit of adventure?" He flicked a switch on the dash and the wipers began to swish back and forth. "How long did you live in England?"

Her head snapped around. "Where did that come from?"

"My snoopy nature again. A lady who calls windshields 'windscreens' and who has an English twist in her speech tends to make me ask questions. Are you English?"

"Half. My mother is English. She felt I should have a proper schooling, so I attended school in High Wycombe, in Buckinghamshire. 'Proper' was the key word there. Proper deportment, proper manners, and proper grammar." She didn't add that she had been yanked out of the school when the scandal about her father had exploded in the British press and her father had been called back to Washington, D.C.

Michael slanted a glance at her before returning his attention to the road. "Dragas isn't exactly an English-sounding name."

"My father's family came from Greece. He's an American, and I was born in Washington, D.C."

There was something vaguely familiar about the name Dragas, but Michael couldn't remember where he had heard it or why. "Did your family live in England too?"

The wipers made a hypnotic, metronomelike sound that mingled with the background noise of raindrops hitting the car. She watched the water slide down the window on her side. "My parents lived in London. Once I started school I saw them only occasionally."

"Must have been lonely for you."

She shrugged. "I was used to it. My parents traveled a great deal, and they didn't want to uproot me too often. At least when I went to the girls' school in England I was able to go home on weekends. High Wycombe is about thirty miles from London. When I went to school in Switzerland, I only saw my parents on holidays."

That was enough about her. She decided to change the subject. "I thought I was supposed to be getting to know you during this little ride. All I know about you is that you own a rare car and your uncle is Judge Dare."

Michael wasn't ready to divulge his occupation yet. What little ground he had gained with her would be lost once she discovered his hated profession.

He was saved from having to answer when she saw where they were going. "This isn't the way to the Embarcadero," she said. "Why didn't you tell me you didn't know where you were going? I would have given you directions."

"I know where I'm going," he answered calmly.

Diana frowned. She knew where he was going too. He was driving toward the Golden Gate Bridge, which would take them to Sausalito. She shrugged. If he wanted to drive her home, that was his choice. His car was certainly more comfortable than the ferry would be, especially since her clothing was damp and the air was chilly. One lesson she had learned as she grew up was that although there were certain situations she couldn't control or change, she could control her reaction to them. Short of jumping out of his car, there wasn't anything she could do but sit back and enjoy the chauffeured ride.

The righteous indignation Michael had been expecting never came. He almost wished she would protest and get it over with. Finally he couldn't stand the silence. "Well?"

"Well what?"

"Aren't you going to object to the fact that I'm taking you home instead of just dropping you off at the Ferry Building, like you asked?"

"Would anything I say make you turn the car around?"

"No."

"Then why should I bother?"

"Beats me," he mumbled distractedly. So far she hadn't done anything the way he expected, so he shouldn't be surprised when she continued to act in her own way. The rain had let up from a heavy downpour to a fine drizzle, so he turned off the wipers. After a long, thoughtful pause, he said, "You are one cool lady, Diana Dragas."

She folded her arms across her chest, running her hands up and down them to warm them. "I'm one freezing lady."

A flick of a switch and hot air rushed out of the heater. "Is that better?"

"Yes, thanks."

They crossed the Golden Gate Bridge, heading toward the rainbow-painted entrance of the Waldo Tunnel. Michael didn't ask for directions until he was driving on Bridgeway, the main street of downtown Sausalito.

"Turn off onto Gate Five Road," Diana told him.

If his memory served him correctly, he thought, Gate Five Road would take them to the area where over three hundred houseboats were docked by the waterfront. The collection of floating houses was an expression of the creativity and imagination of their owners and a popular sight for tourists. Moored on Sausalito's waterfront, it was a variety of homes on water, a community of converted barges, tugboats, ferries, and specially designed homes built to float. Some were elaborate, some plain; others bordered on the bizarre, and a few were downright strange. The fact that Diana Dragas lived in one seemed to fit in with the picture of her he was beginning to form in his mind.

He pulled in and parked where she indicated. Gath-

ering her purse and the wet slippers she had taken off,
Diana opened her door. It had stopped raining completely, and a weak sun was trying to break through
the overcast sky. She turned her head in Michael's
direction. He was looking at her, his expression unreadable.

"Would you like a cup of coffee before you return to
San Francisco?" she asked, falling back on the manners instilled in her at an early age. The offer had
nothing to do with wanting him to stay around longer.
At least that was what she told herself.

He didn't answer immediately. His dark eyes studied
hers for a long moment. Then, apparently finding whatever it was he had been looking for, he removed his
keys from the ignition, opened his door, and ordered
her to stay where she was.

He came around to her side of the car and bent down
to lift her up in his arms. Carrying her easily along the
pier, he asked, "Which houseboat is yours?"

Her arm coiled around his neck. "Second from the
end. I can walk, you know."

He smiled as he looked down into her stunning eyes,
only inches from his. "You could get splinters in your
little bare feet."

"I could put my slippers back on. It would be like
walking on liver, but I could manage it."

He laughed. "Don't be so practical. I'm enjoying this."

She had to admit there were worse ways to travel.
His chest moved against her breast when he laughed,
causing electricity to race through her. She was enjoying being in his arms . . . too much.

"You can put me down now," she said, trying to
sound stern. "This is where I live."

His attention had been solely on her, and he stopped
only because of a gate across the entrance to the walk-
way that led to her home. He merely glanced at the
dwelling. It was difficult to think of anything else while
he held her soft body against his own.

"Michael?"

"Hmmm?"

"Are we going to stand here like this all day?"

"We can if you want to." His eyes stayed on hers, his arms tightening around her.

"I think you had better put me down before the sea gulls start hovering, thinking we're a statue."

He lowered her slowly, almost regretfully, releasing her legs first so her lower body could slide down his, keeping her close until she was standing in front of him. The friction of her body rubbing along his sent a ribbon of desire curling around them.

His hands came up to cup her face. "You are one unique lady, Diana."

She could see the gold glints in the depths of his eyes, and couldn't look away. She was oddly breathless, but managed to ask, "Why? Because I live in a houseboat?"

A thumb smoothed across her soft bottom lip. "Among other things."

They stared at each other for a long, sizzling moment, both aware of the strong attraction growing between them.

Finally Michael smiled slowly. "You said something about a cup of coffee?"

"I did."

"Do I get it served out here or do we go inside?"

She laughed. "Well, since the coffee cups and coffee are inside, it would be easier if we joined them rather than asking them to come out here."

"It sounds fine to me." He made an elaborate sweeping gesture with his arm. "After you."

Diana unlocked the gate and led the way to the houseboat. Michael's gaze roamed over the gray-boarded floating house. The architecture was eclectic, a combination of Victorian gingerbread and contemporary glass. The combination shouldn't have worked, but it did. Hanging pots of geraniums and multicolored vines decorated the small porch surrounding the entranceway, and several window boxes were alive with vibrant color from small, blossoming plants. Tiny stained-glass designs hung in the windows.

"Who's your architect? Walt Disney?" Michael asked. His voice mirrored his amazement.

She laughed. "Wait until you see the inside."

She walked through the front door, and he was a few steps behind her, but she suddenly turned around and came back toward him, carrying something in her hand. He watched her go by him, back outside. Now what? he wondered, and followed her.

She was hooking a navy scrap of material onto a line strung at one side of the porch. With several jerks on the line, she raised the pennant until it was at the top of a thin pole and waving gently in the breeze.

This time he didn't even ask what she was doing. A man could only take so many surprises in one day. However, she decided to give him an explanation without having to be asked.

"My neighbors watch my house while I'm gone. When the pennant is up, they know I'm here."

Looking up at the pennant, Michael could see a splash of gold on the dark blue fabric, but couldn't make out what it was. "Is there any special significance to the design on the pennant?"

For the first time since he had met her, Diana looked slightly embarrassed. "It's a Grecian woman in flowing robes reclining on the moon. It's supposed to represent Diana, the moon goddess. My godfather is an artist, and he painted it for me."

"I thought Diana was the huntress."

She passed him to go back into the house. "That too. She was a busy lady. Come in. I'll fix that coffee I promised you."

With one last glance at the pennant, Michael entered her house. He took two steps, then stopped to gape at the large room.

Good Lord! he thought. There were no walls. Whoever had designed the interior must have had a thing for wide-open spaces. No walls separated one area from another. The kitchen was at one end, with a small dining table several feet away from the counter. Huge plants divided the kitchen from the living area, which was in the center of the houseboat. A couch and several chairs were casually arranged to face a large window displaying a wide view of Richardson Bay. There were more plants and several occasional tables scattered among the heavier furniture. A Japanese folding screen blocked off the bedroom area from the rest of the room.

He brought his bemused gaze back to Diana, who was standing at the kitchen counter. She was measuring coffee beans. She dumped them into a large chrome piece of equipment, pushed a switch, and a whirring sound told him the beans were being ground. She poured the grounds into a cylinder-shaped part of the gadget and water into another section. She flicked a different switch and a variety of noises emanated from the unusual appliance.

Leaning against the doorframe, he asked, "What are you doing?"

"Making coffee."

"Is that all that thing does is make coffee?"

"Yes. What did you expect it to do?"

He shrugged. "Beats me. It looks like it's capable of doing whatever it wants."

"You don't sound like you approve. Don't you like gadgets?"

"I've never thought much about them. But then, since I met you, I've had to consider a number of things I never thought of before. It just seems your coffee maker is like using a boulder to crack walnuts. A mite oversized for the job it has to do."

She smiled at him. "Considering your taste in cars, I

thought you might be prejudiced against newfangled inventions."

"I'm open to any suggestions to update my outlook."

She paused, trying to figure out what the odd gleam in his dark eyes meant. "I'll pass. My specialty is languages. I'm not qualified to teach anything else."

Before he could reply, she walked back over to the coffee maker. Looking over her shoulder, she nodded at his feet. "Take your shoes off."

In a wary, almost belligerent voice, he asked, "Why?"

"Because they're wet. I can put them in the shoe dryer." When he didn't move, she shrugged. "If you prefer to squelch around in soggy shoes, suit yourself."

Resigned, he slipped off his shoes, and she took them from him. Bending down to one of the lower cabinets in the kitchen, she withdrew another strange appliance. She set it on the counter and plugged it in. His shoes were placed on two prongs sticking out of the base, and a red light came on when she depressed a switch.

"You seem to have a gadget for everything," he said.

She grinned. "Just about. I like gadgets."

She pushed another switch on the coffee maker, and gestured toward the living area. "Have a seat. The coffee will be ready in a minute. I want to change out of these wet clothes."

She paused at a small answering machine sitting by the phone on a narrow table, rewound the tape, and began to play the messages back.

Michael's eyes followed her as she disappeared behind the ornate screen. Then he slowly walked over to the window.

There were only three messages. Two were in different languages. The last one was from the agency she worked out of, informing her of an assignment in two weeks. It was another courtroom appearance, this time to translate for the plaintiff, who spoke only German. The machine clicked off.

As Michael looked out across the bay, he could hear the rustling of clothing: a zipper lowering, material sliding over skin. His mind conjured up images to go with the tantalizing sounds, and he felt the tightening of his body. Lord, she didn't even have to be in the same room. He closed his eyes, then quickly opened them again and began pacing around the room, looking for something to take his mind off the activity behind the screen.

He stopped by a card table, where a jigsaw puzzle was in progress. Jelly beans. The whole darn thing was a mass of jelly beans. He idly put in a couple of pieces and wandered on.

Stopping in front of a large bookshelf, he read some of the titles. There were complete collections of Charles Dickens and P. G. Wodehouse, many books with incomprehensible foreign titles, and a selection of mystery novels mixed in with a variety of cookbooks. Returning his attention to the room, he saw a stereo and an assortment of record albums leaning precariously alongside it, but there was something missing. Then he realized what it was. There was no television set. There could have been one in her bedroom, but he doubted it.

He wondered what she would think of the wall in the living room of his apartment that held a large television, a video recorder, and assorted film equipment he used in his work. Probably not much.

He frowned. She didn't own a television and she hated journalists. There had to be a reason, and he was determined to find out what it was. How ironic, he thought, that the most important thing in his life—his career—was the one thing he couldn't discuss with Diana. The woman had captured his imagination and stirred his body with a mere smile, and she hated what he did for a living.

He was pouring himself a cup of coffee, wishing it were something stronger although it was only one o'clock in the afternoon, when Diana appeared from behind the screen. She had changed into a pair of jeans and a large white pullover knit top. Her feet were bare. It was the third outfit he had seen her wearing that day . . . and he wanted to remove every stitch.

He handed her the cup of coffee he had just poured. When he filled another earthenware mug for himself, he was surprised to see his hand was shaking. Turning back to her, he asked. "Feeling better?"

"Decidedly more comfortable and dry. My mother abhors my hoyden clothing," she said in a strong upper-class English accent, indicating her clothing with a flourish of her hand. As she walked toward the living area, she added in her own voice, "I'm afraid I've been rather a trial to my mother. She kept drilling deportment, manners, and the Queen's English into me, hoping I would absorb the basics of behavior for a properly-brought-up young lady. It worked up to a point. I suppose that's why I chose to live here. No one expects me to be anything other than what I am. I can be myself."

He sat down on the couch. "And that's important to you?"

"Being myself? Yes. It's much more comfortable." She sat in one of the easy chairs across from him, crossing one jean-clad leg over the other, looking informally elegant without effort.

"What were you before you became yourself?"

A shadow crossed her face so briefly, Michael wasn't sure he had seen it. Her reply was vague. "Not myself."

"Would you care to explain that?"

"I was what everyone else wanted me to be. I was always supervised, first by a nanny, then a governess, later schoolmistresses, always by my mother. I was constantly being told what to do, when to do it, and how to go about it."

"So now you're a liberated woman?"

She shrugged. "If being liberated means freedom of

choice, then yes, I suppose I am." She met his eyes squarely. "I don't like being told what to do."

Leaning forward, he rested his arms on his knees. "Everyone takes orders at one time or another. We all have rules to follow in our work. We're told to pay our taxes, pay our bills on time, to show up for work. No one has complete freedom."

"I'm not talking about those kind of orders. I'm referring to personal freedom. My days were planned for me down to the slightest details. I had no choice about what I wore, what I ate, where I went, until we came back to the States to live."

"Then what happened?"

Diana looked down into her coffee cup. She wasn't about to tell him why the reins had been loosened by the abrupt changes in her life. "I went to Georgetown University and discovered I was actually capable of making decisions governing my own life." She raised a hand to indicate her surroundings. "I do very well without a keeper, as you can see."

Michael saw plenty, but not enough. What he did see he liked, but he wanted more. And there was more. In his line of work, he studied facial expressions, especially a person's eyes. Diana's vivid eyes had held a trace of wistfulness, of sadness, when she had talked about her past. There were hidden passages in her life she hadn't revealed, and he knew it was too early in their acquaintance to explore them. He could wait.

Leaning back against the upholstered couch, he asked casually, "How long have you lived here?"

"In Sausalito? Almost two years."

"Before that?"

Her eyes narrowed with caution. "You're asking a lot of questions again."

"It's a habit I've gotten into when I want answers." A quick glance at his watch made him set down his cup on a nearby table and stand up. "Unfortunately, I have an appointment to keep that I can't get out of, so the rest of the questions will have to wait."

She didn't move out of her chair. "The questions don't have to be asked at all."

He smiled down at her. "Oh, there will be another time for questions, moon goddess. Could I have my shoes?"

Uncoiling her legs, she stood up. "I doubt there'll be another time," she said as she walked to the kitchen. "The chances of running into each other again in the ladies' loo are slim."

She handed him his shoes, and caught an intent, searching expression in his eyes.

After he had put his shoes back on, she held out her hand. "It's been . . . interesting. Thank you for the ride home."

Michael ignored her hand. He wasn't about to be dismissed with a polite handshake. With slow, deliberate steps, he closed the distance between them, a faint smile softening his hard face. Silently cursing the business commitment that was taking him away from her too soon, he cupped the back of her neck with one hand and lowered his head.

His lips touched hers lightly. When she didn't resist, he deepened the kiss, his other hand finding her hip.

Diana became aware of a multitude of sensations as he changed the slant of his mouth on hers. It was as though she had been a parched desert and he was a river of sensuality flowing over her.

All too soon he raised his head. Staring down into her eyes, he took a deep, ragged breath and smiled. Then he left her without saying anything more about seeing her again.

Feeling disturbed, Diana watched him as he closed the gate behind him and strode away without once looking back. Slowly she turned and walked over to the window facing the bay. Staring at nothing in particular, she thought about the disturbing reaction she had to his kiss, feeling both apprehensive and exhilarated as she remembered the feel of his mouth on hers.

Damn him. She had finally found some peace in her life, and her instincts were screaming to beware of Michael Dare.

Maybe she was worrying needlessly. Maybe she would never see him again. Maybe the reaction to his kiss was just a fluke, a response to the unusual circumstances of their meeting.

She sighed, remembering the gleam of desire in his dark eyes.

Maybe it would snow in July.

Two

The recreational center was located in a rather rough neighborhood of San Francisco. Diana's arrangement with the city was to teach English to high-school students who had immigrated to San Francisco with their parents and were having difficulty with their schoolwork because of their lack of English-language skills.

For the most part, the teenagers were good kids, although some had gigantic chips on their shoulders caused by life, their parents, by being uprooted from their homes and dropped into a strange place with strange ways. Having been a new kid in strange places herself, Diana knew how the teenagers were thinking and feeling, accepting their belligerence as their reaction to their new environment.

The teenagers' normal dislike of any authority figure carried over on to her until she managed to get through to them that she was there to help them, not dictate to them. When they realized she wasn't shocked by their outlandish clothing and obscene language, they began to look at her as someone other than one of the adults who preached to them and criticized them endlessly. She had won them over gradually, and they were now responding to her instruction.

The students were a continuing challenge, and she rather enjoyed pitting her skills against theirs, although she'd barely made it alive through the first session.

One of the legs of her chair had been loosened, a live mouse had startled her when she opened a desk drawer, and some of the words they had used when addressing her would have made a sailor blush. When she had signed the contract with the city to teach remedial English, she hadn't realized basic survival techniques would be useful. Now the students no longer tried dirty tricks or used the shocking language around her. In fact, they had become decidedly protective of her.

The class began at four in the afternoon, giving the students time to get there after their regular school. On Friday Diana had dismissed everyone at five o'clock, but had been delayed by one of the girls, who had to fill out a health form and needed help.

When Diana finally was able to leave the building, she saw two men walking toward her. She immediately knew who, or, more precisely, what, they were. Reporters.

One of them was carrying the inevitable camera, while the other man had a tape recorder ready. The minute she spotted them, she tried to evade them by walking the other way, but she wasn't quick enough. They had seen her too.

Four of her students were lingering around the front of the building, so she had no choice but to stop when one of the men called out her name. Her students wouldn't understand why she would run away when the two men obviously wanted to talk to her. She stopped and faced them. "Miss Dragas," said the man with the tape recorder, "We would like to interview you for *Vista* magazine. Our readers would like to read about your daring rescue of a judge."

She shook her head and turned to walk away, but the man stepped in front of her, blocking her path.

She glared at him. "I don't give interviews."

"Do you think that's fair to the public?" he asked aggressively.

"As fair as hounding people who don't want to be on

public display," she snapped angrily, trying once again to move around him.

He sidestepped in front of her. "The public has a right to know what happened in that courtroom. Think of how the story will inspire others to stand up to criminals."

"Criminals?" she asked scoffingly. "He was a frightened, deaf sixteen-year-old boy who has been brought up in a violent environment. He reacted out of fear and took the one step he understood. Violence. Now, go away. If you're so desperate to interview someone, go to City Hall and interview one of the politicians. They love to talk to reporters."

Out of the corner of her eye, she saw the four boys looking her way and edging closer. When she again tried to walk away and the reporters again stopped her by moving in front of her, the boys decided to take action.

With their long hair and black leather jackets, they were unlikely knights in shining armor, but they set about to rescue her just the same. They moved forward as a threatening mass of youthful reprisal. Diana was relieved they were on her side. If she hadn't known them, they would have scared her silly.

"These guys bothering you, Miz Dragas?" one of the boys asked.

She attempted to defuse the explosive situation before the boys took action. "It's all right, Antonio. They were just leaving."

The reporter eyed the boys warily, but he obviously didn't have the sense of a gnat. "We aren't leaving until we get our story."

"I have nothing to say." Diana started past him, but the reporter proved he was not only persistent but also extremely stupid, by grasping her arm to restrain her.

Antonio moved quickly. Gripping the man's wrist, the muscular youth applied enough pressure to persuade the reporter to release Diana. "You keep your hands off the lady, man."

The other three boys moved closer, their bodies tensed. The cameraman raised his camera to film the scene, but Antonio, keeping his dark gaze on the reporter, pushed the camera away. Obviously wanting to protect the expensive equipment, the cameraman shoved Antonio, attempting to get him away from the camera.

Antonio shoved back. He turned the air blue with descriptive phrases in both English and Italian dealing with the cameraman's anatomy and parents. The reporter, like the idiot Diana had suspected he was, entered the fray, yelling back at Antonio and pushing one of the other boys away.

Diana didn't want the boys to get into any trouble because of her, so she stepped into the middle of the fracas to separate the combatants.

At that moment Michael arrived at the recreational center, looking for Diana. He had a scowl on his face as he gazed around the neighborhood, wondering what in the world she was doing in this rough area of the city. He didn't pay much attention to the group in front of the center until he spotted Diana smack dab in the middle of it, surrounded by two men and some rough-looking teenagers, all of whom were yelling and shoving one another. His scowl deepened. It seemed he was destined to extract her from crowds.

He slammed on his brakes and shoved open his door, leaving his car parked in the street. Plowing through the bodies, he clamped a hand around Diana's arm, and yanked her toward him, then pushed her behind him as he faced the men and boys.

"She's with me," he said.

One of the boys, who looked like a juvenile member of the Hell's Angels, challenged him. "Who sez, man?" he asked in heavily accented English and a knife suddenly appeared in his hands.

Diana tried to come out from behind Michael, but his hand kept her in place. "Take my word for it," he said. His voice was quiet and deadly.

"Michael—" Diana began.

"Stay out of this, Diana."

The reporter saw the knife and began backing away, not even looking at Michael. Catching his cameraman's attention, he gave a jerk of his head, which meant, in anyone's language, to get the hell out of there.

They slunk away, leaving Michael alone to confront the pack.

Diana squirmed against Michael's hold on her. If he'd just let her move out from behind him to talk to the boys . . .

"Dammit, Diana," he said. "Stay still. I'll handle this."

This was ridiculous, she thought. The boys were trying to protect her, Michael was trying to protect her, and she was trying to protect Michael. She managed to peek around him, and saw the boys taking slow, deliberate steps toward Michael, spreading out to cover each side. Four menacing switchblades were waving about, adding an obvious danger to an already explosive situation. It was time to end this.

Instead of pulling away, she leaned against Michael's back, slipping her arms around his waist. This was one of those occasions when actions would have to speak louder than words, she decided. When her breasts pressed against his broad back, she felt Michael stiffen in surprise.

Her possessive gesture did the trick. Antonio and his friends visibly backed off.

"Hey, Miz Dragas," Antonio said. "You know diz guy?"

Michael loosened his hold on her enough to allow him room to move her in front of him without turning his back on the boys. Then he wrapped his arms around her, holding her against him, her back to his front. Posing a similar question in better English, he asked, "Do you know these guys?"

"Yes. They're some of my students." She nodded to Antonio. "Thanks, Antonio. I appreciate your help with those two men. As you can see, I don't need rescuing from this man." She was about to introduce Michael, when the boy next to Antonio spoke up.

"Hey, he's that guy on TV." Seeing the blank faces around him he explained, "Remember that show we had to watch and make a report on for sociology? That's the guy who talked during the whole show."

Michael felt Diana tense. Damn. He had been afraid this was going to happen, but he hadn't expected it so soon. The boys approached them and began to ask him questions. One even asked for an autograph, the past hostilities forgotten. His car came under discussion next, and Michael brought Diana with him as he and the boys walked over to his car. They asked him all about the motor, how fast it would go, and whether it was good for cruisin' chicks. He furnished the information concerning the speed and the type of motor, but didn't reply to the question concerning "chicks."

Luckily there wasn't much traffic as they stood in the road by his car. Leaving his left hand free to sign the odd bits of paper shoved at him, Michael kept his right arm around Diana's waist to keep her from walking away. One glance at her stormy eyes was enough to give him an indication of her feelings. He was definitely not her favorite person at the moment. His arm tightened. He needed to explain about his job, and he couldn't if she took off.

After several "Hey, man's" and slaps on the back, the boys sauntered off to find other excitement or make some of their own.

Michael looked down at Diana. Her eyes were cold turquoise ice. He was in trouble.

"Who were those two men?" he asked.

"Reporters. The boys were . . . discouraging them."

"You don't seem to be as impressed with my credentials as those boys were."

She tried to move away from him, but his arm only tightened around her waist. "You're very perceptive, for a television commentator."

"Journalist," he corrected her, "but I prefer the word *commentator* to several other choices I expected you to use."

"I will if you like," she said acidly. "In fact, I can say bastard in six different languages." Her hand pried at his fingers, still clamped on her waist. "You can let me go now, TV man."

"No, I don't think I can."

Diana's gaze locked with his. She was puzzled by his serious tone, the sober expression in his eyes. Each movement he made had an odd grace, a lithe charm that sent waves of sheer pleasure through her. Why couldn't he have been a doctor, a lawyer, a ditchdigger? Anything but a journalist. Why did he have to appeal to her in a way no other man had appealed to her? Her heart raced whenever she looked at him. His touch sent flames licking along her veins.

"Thanks for the rescue," she said, "but I don't talk to journalists or commentators, or whatever you choose to call yourself. I'm not real wild about being lied to, either. You should have told me."

He apparently heard her, but his question didn't have anything to do with what she had said. "Why did you put your arms around me earlier?"

His breath was warm on her skin, distracting her. She had to concentrate on her answer so he wouldn't get the wrong idea about her motives and think she had wanted to be close to him. "I had to get your attention and show the boys I knew you. It was the only thing I could think of at the time, since you ignored everything I said. Silly of me, but I didn't want them to hurt you. But then I didn't know you were in the same exalted profession as those other two leeches."

Smiling slowly, he murmured, "Your move was very effective. I almost forgot about the lads in leather when I felt your hands on me."

"Consider it my one good deed for the day. Don't hold your breath waiting for it to happen again."

He took her hand and walked her around to the passenger side of his car. "So where would you like to have dinner?"

"Look, you imbecilic twit!" she snapped. "I'm trying to tell you to get lost. I don't plan on having dinner with you. I don't even want to talk to you."

He opened the car door. "That's too bad, because that's exactly what we're going to do. Talk."

She grabbed onto the frame of the door. "So I can answer some of your questions? No, thanks, Mr. Journalist. I've answered questions before from your kind. I didn't like it much."

"For a lady who supposedly understands so many languages," he said, "you appear a little muddled when it comes to certain English words. Talk means conversing, dialogue, conversation, usually involving two or more people, although I have a great-aunt who mumbles to herself a great deal when she cooks or works in her garden, but she's an exception."

"When journalists talk, it usually turns into an interrogation. I'll pass."

His gaze dwelled on her lips before returning to her eyes. "Interrogations have nothing to do with the way we will be communicating."

"I knocked a gun out of a sixteen-year-old deaf boy's hand. I didn't single-handedly catch the number-one most-wanted man in America. Surely you can't be that desperate for a story."

His voice became hard and gritty. "Don't be so damn critical of something you know nothing about. You haven't the faintest idea what kind of work I do. Now, park your lovely rear end in my car so we can leave."

She parked her lovely rear end, refusing to dwell on why she was doing as he ordered. Maybe it was the injured pride she had heard in his voice when he defended his work. Perhaps she had lashed out unfairly, condemning him and his work blindly without having witnessed the type of programs he was producing. There was enough doubt mixed with curiosity to give her the excuse to spend more time with him. Still, she felt a familiar resentment over his bossing her around. When he parked near a restaurant on California Street, she told herself she would have just walked away if she weren't so darned intrigued by this blasted man.

They were shown to a table covered with crisp white linen and secluded enough to allow private conversation. A waiter appeared almost immediately, and, not particularly hungry, they each ordered a shrimp salad and a glass of wine.

Michael sat back in his chair, watching Diana look around the restaurant. The warmth, the friendliness, the humor he had seen the day he met her were noticeably absent. When her eyes finally came back to him, he reached into the pocket of his sport jacket and withdrew a legal-sized envelope.

He held it out to her. "Here. I want you to read this."

Diana had expected words, not paper. Her fingers closed around the envelope. "What is it?"

"You'll find out when you read it."

The paper crackled as she unfolded a couple of typed pages. In a column on the left, were dates followed by descriptions of the type of work Michael had been involved in during that period of time. It was a résumé of his work history. She discovered he had been in advertising before becoming a correspondent in the Middle East, had been a network newscaster for several years after being a local newscaster in Los Angeles, then had switched to being a producer/director of documentaries, even occasionally narrating and appearing in them. The subjects of the documentaries ranged from buried treasure, to the Mayan culture, to lighthouses along the Eastern Shore, to his latest program, about homeless street people.

After reading to the end of the second page, she looked up. "Do you usually carry around a list of your credits?"

"Only when I meet dark-haired linguists who show a marked distaste for the field of journalism. I called the agency I heard on your answering machine yesterday, and they told me where you were. I was going to explain to you about my work, but those boys beat me to it."

"If this"—she rustled the papers in her hand—"is supposed to impress me, I—"

"It's supposed to inform," he interrupted impatiently, "the same as my programs are supposed to do." He leaned forward, his forearms on the table. "Not to intrude or invade, but inform. I don't badger people or pressure them into talking to me. That's not how I work. A great deal of research is done to make sure all the facts are correct before one reel of tape is made. I don't embroider facts or stretch them to fit any given pattern. I would prefer not to appear in any of the programs, but the network seems to think I'm a recognizable draw for audiences, so they use me. I have to make certain compromises like that, but if the facts aren't honest or true, I don't do it. That's one compromise I won't make."

Diana studied the serious expression in his eyes. Then she folded the papers and stuffed them back in the envelope to give herself something to do while she thought about what he had said.

Finally raising her eyes, she asked quietly, "Why are you making such a big deal out of this?"

"Because you are. You don't like journalists, and I'm a journalist. Being a journalist is what I do. It's an important part of my life, a part of me. I have to change your opinion."

She laid the envelope on his side of the table. "You don't impress me as the type of man who needs approval from everyone he meets."

"I don't care if everyone approves," he said firmly. "Only you."

Sitting back in her chair, she stared at the man

across from her. He kept surprising her. It really seemed to matter to him what she thought of him. What also surprised her was her willingness to be persuaded not to prejudge him on the basis of his line of work.

She smiled weakly. "I've made wrong assumptions about you since we've met. My first clue that you didn't fit the mold I had formed for you was discovering you drive an antique." She lifted her chin and looked directly at him, adding sincerely, "I'm not so pigheaded I can't admit there are good and bad members of every profession. Perhaps you're one of the exceptions in the field of journalism."

Michael felt a flood of relief, and was alarmed at the strength of his feelings. She was going to meet him halfway. With reservations, but at least he was being given a chance. He wasn't about to do anything to lose that chance, but he still had to step carefully along the path he planned to walk with her. One misstep, one stumble, and he would fall into the category of despised journalists.

He made a promise to himself to learn why she hated journalists in general. He couldn't fight an enemy without knowing who or what it was.

The waiter plunked down their salads and glasses of wine, then hurried off. His obvious haste made Diana wonder if he had a quota to fill for serving the most customers in a certain amount of time. It was either that or the customers were all on the verge of starvation and he felt it his supreme duty to feed them as quickly as humanly possible.

Michael lifted his glass. "To waiters who take great pride in their work."

Smiling, she lifted her glass and clinked it against his. "And with such style. Only one shrimp jumped off my plate."

Poking a rubbery shrimp with his fork, Michael said, "Maybe it tried to commit suicide."

She ignored her plate. Even though she had only

munched on an apple for lunch, she wasn't hungry. Food wasn't on her mind, but Michael Dare was, as he had been since she had met him the day before. What was it about him that disturbed her in such a frightening, exhilarating way?

He looked up and caught her pensive expression. Setting down his fork, he also gave up any pretense of eating. What he would rather do was take her back to his apartment to get rid of the ache in his loins. He wasn't even touching her and his body had tightened with need.

"Next time," he said, his voice low and husky, "we'll go to a French restaurant, so you can translate the menu for me. I usually have to point and hope I don't order liver and onions."

So there was to be a next time? she mused. He seemed very confident of that. She couldn't imagine he had to struggle to get what he wanted. Ever. His air of confidence came to him as naturally as breathing.

He was obviously expecting her to say something, so she went along with the subject of languages. "Basic survival was why I decided I had better learn a foreign language. I discovered hand signals and desperate gestures weren't going to work when I tried to find out where the ladies' room was in a department store in Germany. Instead of just learning key phrases like how much does it cost and where's the bathroom, I went the whole route, learning to speak and write the language wherever we lived."

England and now Germany, he thought. Carefully phrasing his next question so it wouldn't appear to be one, he said, "You've apparently traveled a great deal."

She watched him intently. "My father was in the diplomatic corps." There was no sign Michael had made the connection between Dragas and diplomat, so she continued. "I found I had a knack for languages, and ended up able to speak and write fluent German, French, Italian, Spanish, and Greek."

A shadowy memory wavered in the back of his mind, yet Michael couldn't bring it out into the light. Dragas. A diplomat. There was something vaguely familiar about the two, but he couldn't pin it down.

"I suppose," he said, "it was easier to learn a language while living in the country where the language was spoken than out of books."

She sipped her wine, and replied lightly, "It made shopping a lot easier."

"And easier to find the ladies' rest room," he tacked on.

She smiled. "That too."

"And easier to understand propositions from the men you dated, so you could say no."

She tilted her head to one side, her smile tugging at a corner of her soft mouth. "What makes you think I said no?"

"Wishful thinking." His scowl was mostly from frustration. It was difficult to get the information he wanted without asking direct questions. She didn't like questions from journalists. To hell with it. He had to know.

"Did you say no?"

"No."

Keeping his expression blank, he swallowed his disappointment. Or was it regret? No. It was pure jealousy that some other man or men had touched her. What had he expected? She was an attractive, sensual woman. Of course there had been other men in her life. It was ridiculous to feel this possessive desire to have her exclusively. He was so deep in thought, he almost didn't hear her next words.

"I haven't had to say no."

He stared at her. "What do you mean?" He was actually holding his breath for her answer.

"I've never found a man interesting enough to cause me to commit myself to an intimate relationship, and I'm not into casual affairs. I guess it's my fastidious upbringing." She smiled at his stunned expression.

"You must travel in faster social circles than I do if you're so shocked. There are a lot of women out there who don't hop into bed at the snap of a man's fingers."

He looked at her curiously. "What would happen if I snapped my fingers now?"

"You would probably get the waiter," she said dryly.

He laughed. "But not you, right?"

"I just told you. I don't go in for casual affairs. You'll have to snap your fingers in some other woman's direction."

Michael was no longer amused. "Making love with you would be anything but casual."

It was suddenly very warm in the restaurant, Diana thought. She was mesmerized by the disturbing heat in his eyes, feeling a responding flame flicker through her. The temptation to find out if he was right was stronger than she was comfortable with, so she dismissed it.

"Let me put it this way," she said. "You've obviously had a lot of experience with casual affairs, and I haven't had any. There isn't a great deal of common ground there to warrant a long drawn-out discussion, so let's change this fascinating subject."

Michael looked as if he were all set to continue the fascinating subject, but a woman approached the table at that moment, wanting his autograph.

The woman's permed hair fairly bristled with excitement. "I told Elsie it was you, Mr. Dare. I never forget a face. She said it couldn't possibly be you, but I said you have to eat, same as anyone else, so why not here?" Accepting the autographed napkin, she shook his hand as though pumping a well, and gushed, "It is a thrill to meet you, Mr. Dare. I do enjoy your programs, especially that one about street people. It made me cry. It really did."

Michael thanked her warmly, at the same time discouraging her from lingering longer. He was polite but firm, sending the woman on her way back to the skeptical Elsie with his autograph clutched in her hand.

When they were alone once again, Diana murmured, "Very nicely done. Does this sort of thing happen often?"

"Often enough."

"Why did you switch from being a newscaster to doing documentaries? I would think there would be more exposure on national television. Every night you would be in everyone's living room."

"Not in yours. You don't own a television set."

"I never got into the habit of watching television. I've always been too busy. When I first moved to Sausalito, I couldn't afford to buy one, and when I could, I found I didn't really want one. When I'm home I usually read or have translations to work on in the evenings. You didn't answer my question."

He sat back in his chair. "The nightly news programs were too instant, too temporary. I reported the daily news, and then twenty-four hours later another day's highlights of disasters, political decisions, deaths. I wanted to do something with more depth. Something more permanent."

There was more depth to Michael as well, she thought. "What type of program are you involved in now?"

He was about to tell her about his current project when the bill for their meal floated down onto the table as the waiter made a fleeting pass by them.

Laugh lines deepened the corners of Michael's eyes as he grinned at Diana and held up the bill. "We have been served our walking papers."

"I think Swifty would prefer our running to the nearest exit. The rest of the world is in slow motion compared to him." Placing her napkin on the table, she added, "As much as I hate to give Swifty the satisfaction of seeing our backs go out the door, I should be catching the next ferry."

"What's your hurry? I can drive you home later."

She shook her head. "That's not necessary." She

glanced at her watch. "There's a ferry due in twenty minutes."

He looked at her plate. "You haven't eaten anything."

She looked at his. "Neither have you."

"I wonder if it's for the same reason," he murmured cryptically. Leaning back in his chair, he suggested, "We could go somewhere else. To a place where the service is slower and the food is more appetizing than plastic shrimp."

"I can't. I promised to meet a friend in Sausalito, and I have to leave now or I'll be late."

If Michael was disappointed, he hid it very well. With a nod of agreement, he pushed back his chair, his expression unreadable.

When they arrived at the landing, the ferry was about ten minutes away and could be seen slowly approaching. Michael waited beside Diana, even though she had told him he didn't have to.

His gaze on the ferry as it drifted across the water, he asked quietly, "Who's your friend?"

She brushed away the hair that had blown across her face. "What friend?"

"The one you're meeting later."

He had turned to look at her, but now she was watching the ferry, a slight frown in her eyes and around her mouth. "A friend with a problem."

"Is he important to you? This friend with a problem?"

She met his gaze. "Yes, *she* is. Our parents have been friends for as long as I can remember. In fact, they live in the houseboat next to mine. Nicole has finally agreed to come down from the mountains for a short visit. It's been over a year since I've seen her, and it may be another year before she will come again."

His gaze returned to the approaching ferry. "When can I see you?"

"Michael . . ." she said hesitantly.

"Diana . . ." He mimicked her tone of weary resignation. He turned toward her and cupped her chin with his hand. "I want to see you again," he said seriously, then suddenly he smiled. "I'm really not all that awful, even though I'm a journalist. When I come for you, you can frisk me for tape recorders and note pads. In fact, I insist. I like your hands on me."

Her eyes searched his face, seeing the strength, the humor, the sensuality that drew her to him like steel filings to a magnet.

His thumb ran a slow trail across her bottom lip. "I want to see you again."

Unable to look away, she gave in. "Nicole only stays one night."

"Tomorrow night?"

She smiled. "Eight o'clock?"

"Make it seven. I may be able to last that long."

His hand slid down the side of her face to her neck. The intensity of her response to his light touch made it difficult to breathe, much less speak.

"All right. Seven."

His lips touched hers briefly before he gave her a gentle push toward the ferry. "Seven."

Walking away, Diana muttered to herself, "I hope I know what I'm doing."

Three

Nicole's limp was barely noticeable, which meant her injured leg was better. But her attitude toward men hadn't improved since Diana had seen her last.

"So you're going to go out with this guy tomorrow night even though he's one of those nasty journalists?" Nicole asked.

They were seated in the living area of Diana's houseboat, relaxing and catching up with each other's lives after having dinner with Nicole's parents at their houseboat next door. Diana was slumped casually in the corner of a plump upholstered chair, with her bare feet perched on a matching hassock, and Nicole was sprawled comfortably on the couch, her bad leg stretched out on the cushions. Both women held delicate crystal wineglasses that had been refilled several times.

"You make him sound like some unspeakable fungus," Diana said, keeping her tone light.

"I thought that was how you classified all journalists."

Diana swirled the wine in her glass. "Michael is . . . different."

"That's what they all say," Nicole drawled.

Diana narrowed her eyes in order to clear the myopic, wine-induced fog. "What does who all say?"

Nicole chuckled. "You just massacred the English language as we know it today."

"It's your mother's lethal fruit punch. My tongue is numb."

"So is your brain."

The quiet, bitter statement cut through the pleasant haze surrounding Diana. Sitting up straighter in the chair she asked, "Why? Because I'm going out with one of those horrid creatures you've sworn off? He's not Clay, Nikki." She saw Nicole's face go white. "I'm sorry. That was a low blow." She sighed. "It's just that I'm having a few doubts about my own sanity. I don't need to hear your dire warnings about the male species in general and Michael in particular."

Nicole pushed herself up to a sitting position. Her shining blond hair glimmered in the light from the lamp on the table next to the couch. The black silk shirt and black slacks she wore contrasted dramatically with her porcelain skin and pale hair. Short and slender, Nicole gave a false impression of fragility. But Diana knew that inside her small frame was a core of steel, toughened by her leg injury and the long recovery.

Leaning back against the couch, Nicole sighed heavily. "I don't want you to be hurt." "The way I was" could have been tacked on, but Nicole didn't say those words aloud. It wasn't necessary. Diana was well aware of the emotional pain Nicole had suffered along with her physical injury after the car accident and Clay's desertion.

"I'm only going to spend a couple of hours with an interesting man," she said. "There's nothing serious between us."

Nicole's mouth twisted into a skeptical grimace. "You haven't seen the look you get in your eyes whenever you mention his name. What scares me more than that warm glow is that his line of work crosses over into a danger zone. Don't forget, I was there when those reporters tore into your family like a pack of hungry wolves. I saw the hatred in your eyes when they pounced. Don't tell me you've suddenly decided journalists are swell fellas after all. I won't believe it."

"He does documentaries, not exposés. Even if he was a reporter for one of those unscrupulous tabloids, there's nothing for him to report on. My father is no longer big news and my little stunt in the courtroom is hardly headline material."

"Does he know who your father is, or I should say, was?"

Diana shook her head. "No, I don't think so. It wouldn't matter if he did. My father is no longer in the diplomatic corps, and the scandal involving his friendship with a Russian diplomat is old news."

"Maybe your new friend wants to do a documentary on gay relationships."

"My father is not gay!" Diana said hotly.

Nicole put her hand up in a placating gesture. "I know, I know, but that's what he was accused of, among other things, with that young Russian diplomat. The fact that he was trying to help the man doesn't make a great deal of difference to people who like to wallow in dirt."

"I've had a lot of experience with all different types of approaches from a variety of hungry newshounds. I'll know if Michael is after a story."

"Will you? Or will you be too preoccupied with your emotions to be objective?"

Diana became restless. Getting out of her chair, she walked over to the table her jigsaw puzzle was on and fiddled with a couple of pieces. "You aren't saying anything I haven't already said to myself, Nikki." She turned and looked at her friend. "Why don't you help me finish this wretched puzzle? I'm getting sick of these jelly beans."

"In other words, you want to change the subject."

"I would prefer it, yes." She slanted a gentle look in Nicole's direction. "Would you rather talk about how worried your parents are about you?"

"No." Placing a hand on the arm of the couch, Nicole stood up. Diana saw her grimace slightly, and knew her leg was hurting. "I'd better go back to spend some time with the folks."

"Are you still planning to return to the cabin tomorrow?"

"Yes." Nicole joined her at the table and stared down at the partly finished puzzle. "I saw the director of the art gallery this afternoon and made all the arrangements for the exhibit. I still find it hard to believe anyone would want to buy my paintings. I've never had any training. They were just something to do while waiting for my leg to heal. I don't know why my aunt sent one of them off to that gallery in the first place."

"Because your paintings are charming. There's an innocence about them that appeals to people who are somewhat jaded from today's fast-paced society. Your mother mentioned something about lithographic prints being made of the harvest still life."

"It's a 'flat-perspective primitive,' according to the director of the gallery."

"Really?" Diana chuckled. "Exactly what does that mean?"

"You got me. Since he thinks it will make me a lot of money, he can call it anything he wants to." She fit a piece into the puzzle. "Now I need to get back to my cabin. The gallery wants more paintings than I have ready."

Diana knew another reason Nicole wanted to get back to her mountain retreat. Clay McMasters lived in San Francisco. The chances of running into him in such a large city were slim, but Nicole wasn't ready to tempt fate even a little. Fate hadn't been particularly kind to her in the past, and there was no reason to think it would deal out any favors now. The healing of her physical injury was more rapid than her recovery from the battering her emotions had received. The scars left by Clay would have a better chance of healing if Nicole could understand why he had dropped abruptly out of her life without any explanation after the accident.

Diana's attention returned to the puzzle. "How much time do you have before the exhibit?"

"It's set for November." Nicole found another piece. "That gives me four months to get ready."

"It sounds like you have a new career," Diana said, then asked bluntly, "Are you still having trouble sleeping?"

Nicole's head jerked up. For a moment Diana didn't think she was going to answer, but finally she said, "A little."

"A little what? A little trouble or a little sleep?"

Nicole's mouth twisted. "Leave it alone, Di. I've gone over all this with my parents. I'm all right."

Diana bit her lip to stop herself from asking if Nicole was still resorting to sleeping pills in order to sleep. They had been close friends all their lives, which allowed them to speak frankly with each other, but there was a limit to how far the bonds of friendship could be stretched.

"Glad to hear you're all right," she said.

Changing the subject, Nicole asked, "Do you think my father is well? He seems preoccupied, sort of restless."

"I think he's just bored. Rena says he misses working. Abe had a long run in that last television series, but it's been over four years since he's worked. He thinks the public has forgotten about him."

"He could change careers, the way your father did."

"My father doesn't care for being in the limelight. Yours thrives on it. Dealing in real estate is rather tame compared to being an actor. No one asks for an autograph from the man who sells him a house."

Nicole chuckled. "Mom says every time she opens the refrigerator door, Dad takes a bow as the light goes on."

"That's what I mean. Your father's been an actor over thirty years. He likes applause and all the rest of the perks that go with being a star. It's a bit of a comedown to spend his days quietly on a houseboat or on a golf course instead of on a television or movie set."

Fitting in another piece, Nicole muttered, "These darn puzzle pieces are like peanuts. You can't stop at just one."

"Each time I finish a puzzle, I say never again, but I'm addicted. Do you think they have a jigsaw puzzler's anonymous?"

"I doubt it." Nicole began gathering her purse and jacket. "Let's hope my father doesn't bug your new boyfriend for a spot in one of his shows."

"He's not my boyfriend," Diana said defensively. "Besides, I doubt Michael's planning to do a documentary on retired actors."

At seven o'clock the following evening, Diana had just stepped out of her front door to lower the moongoddess pennant when she saw Michael walking along the pier toward her houseboat. Rena and Abe Piccolo were also strolling along the pier, and it was inevitable that the three would meet. Diana had made the mistake of mentioning Michael and her date with him the previous night. Rena and Abe had been very interested in this development and had said they wanted to meet Michael. Abe had seen several of Michael's programs, and had raved about them.

Diana took her sweet time lowering the pennant. She had the feeling Rena and Abe had been watching for Michael. When they stopped and waited like regal sentries at the gate to her houseboat, she knew she had been right. They took their duty as stand-in parents seriously, and they wanted to check out the guy Diana would be going out with.

Michael recognized Abe Piccolo immediately when he reached the couple obviously waiting for him. As coincidence would have it, Abe was one of the actors on his list of once-famous people no longer active in their professions, people he wanted to interview for his next documentary, entitled, "Where Are They Now?"

He and the Piccolos introduced themselves, and Michael was subjected to a keen-eyed inspection from Diana's neighbors. He, in turn, studied them.

Rena Piccolo was one of those women who accepted her advancing years gracefully. Her graying auburn hair was stylishly but simply cut, and arranged to flatter her porcelain, heart-shaped face. Her green eyes were partly obscured by lightly tinted glasses.

Like his wife, Abe Piccolo was dressed all in white, except for a dark blue ascot around his neck. He was a tall man, his eyes on a level with Michael's, and he gave Michael a sharp look.

"I've seen several of your programs, young man," he said. "You do nice work."

"Thanks," Michael said. "I've seen most of your work, too, Mr. Piccolo. It's a pleasure to meet you."

Diana had finally finished lowering the pennant, but still hesitated to join the others. Give a man enough rope and he'll hang himself, she thought. If Michael was going to turn into a typical journalist, meeting a film legend would set the journalistic wheels in his mind in motion. It was better to find out now than later.

When at last she joined the chattering threesome, she heard Rena invite Michael to their party the following night. "I know it's short notice, but we would love to have you come."

Michael casually slid his arm around Diana's shoulders, the gesture possessive and natural . . . and Abe and Rena noticed.

"Can we let you know?" he asked.

"Of course. You two talk it over. It was a pleasure to meet you, Michael. We hope to see you again tomorrow night."

Abe added in his usual, machine-gun style, "Give me a call. We'll have lunch. Diana can give you our number. We're not in the book."

Michael smiled, but refrained from making a commitment. Looking down at Diana he asked softly, "Are you ready to go?"

The intimate look in his eyes was warm and inviting. She nodded, and said good night to the Piccolos.

During the drive over the Golden Gate Bridge, Diana and Michael got into a friendly argument about the ending of a movie Abe Piccolo had starred in. She thought the ending had left too many questions unanswered, and his opinion was that the ending was supposed to make the audience use its imagination. Diana was so absorbed in debating the issue, she didn't pay much attention to where they were going. The first indication that they had arrived at their destination was when Michael shut off the engine.

Since she had no idea where Michael planned to take her, she had played it safe and worn her good old basic-black dress. It was appropriate for most places. It was certainly appropriate for where Michael had decided to take her.

His apartment.

"Ah . . . Michael," she said cautiously, seeing that they were parked in front of what was obviously an apartment building. "For fear of sounding terribly unoriginal, I'm not that kind of girl."

Michael made a scolding sound with his tongue. "You do jump to some rather nasty conclusions about me."

"This isn't your apartment?"

"It's my apartment, but we're only going to have dinner." He smiled. "Of course, if you plan to search me for a tape recorder, I can't promise not to react to the feel of your hands on me."

That was odd, she thought. All of a sudden her fingers tingled at the thought of roaming over his splendid body. Clearing her throat, she managed to ask, "Have you anything against restaurants?"

"No," he replied calmly. "Do you?"

"I rather fancy them."

"I see I'm going to have to give you an incentive to

come up to my apartment instead of your insisting on going to a restaurant."

She shifted slightly so she could see his face better. "This I've got to hear."

His sigh was exaggerated, as if he were feeling greatly put-upon. "Last Christmas my great-aunt, the one who chats to herself, gave me a peculiar thingamajig that I politely thanked her for and shoved away in the back of a cupboard as soon as she left."

He paused, giving Diana time to comment if she chose, but she was showing a marked lack of curiosity. "After I saw how you like gadgets, I dug it out. I thought you might like to try it out tonight. If it works, we will feast on homemade fettuccine. If it doesn't work, we'll have to settle for a peanut butter sandwich or a frozen pizza."

After a few minutes had passed, Diana finally spoke. "So if I want something to eat, I have to cook it?"

He couldn't see her face clearly in the dark but he heard the amusement in her voice. "I'll help. I don't expect you to do it all yourself."

There was another long pause, then she said, "It seems to me we had better get started in that case."

He chuckled. She was something else, he thought. He couldn't imagine another woman like her. *He* certainly had never run across any woman like her before. Just when he expected a battle, she surrendered. When he didn't expect one, she fought him. Keeping up with her was definitely a challenge.

He directed her toward the kitchen as soon as they entered his apartment. He poured them each some wine and they began, chopping spinach, mixing, kneading, and rolling out dough for the pasta in between frequent pauses to read the instructions. Thanks to those comprehensive instructions and a mountain of ingredients, they produced a reasonable facsimile of green pasta.

Michael insisted on eating in the formal dining room,

saying the kitchen resembled a battle zone. Diana agreed. Every inch of the small table in the kitchen was covered with flour, bowls, and the pasta-making machine.

The polished cherry table in the dining room was already set with two linen place mats, navy cloth napkins, silverware, and pewter wine goblets. Michael lit the candles in the matching pewter candlesticks in the center of the table. While Diana set their filled plates down on the place mats, he turned the light switch near the doorway, and the glow from the chandelier dimmed.

Seeing the suspicious look Diana sent his way, he smiled. "I'm a sucker for atmosphere."

And she was a sucker to be going along with him, she told herself. "I thought maybe you preferred lowering the lights so you didn't have to look at what you were eating."

After pouring the wine he had brought in from the kitchen, he sat across from her. He looked down at his plate, then at her. "Ladies first."

Picking up a fork, she stabbed at the green noodles. "It just sort of lies there."

Seeing she wasn't going to try it, he twirled his fork into the noodles and bravely went first. A moment later he exclaimed in surprise, "It's good."

It was Diana's turn. After the first mouthful she took another, and then another. "It's delicious."

Before they were through, they had each had a second helping. When their plates were finally empty and they were full, Diana leaned back in her chair and asked, "I don't suppose your great-aunt gave you anything that would instantly clean up the kitchen, did she?"

"I'm afraid not. I have plenty of trash bags. If worse comes to worst, we'll just toss everything in them and let the garbage man take it away."

A few minutes later they were in the kitchen, attempting to clean up the mess they had made. With a large dish towel wrapped around his waist, Michael washed his hands at the sink.

"I'm going to hint to my great-aunt to get me a toaster next Christmas. At least I know how that works."

"You're just cranky because you cut your finger chopping up the spinach."

"Spinach. I never knew why green noodles were green. Although I can't say I've stayed awake nights wondering about it."

"Now you know why your great-aunt gave you this pasta maker, to improve your mind."

"To starve me." Wiping his hands on a towel, he walked over to where she was putting their plates into the dishwasher. "It took us over two hours to make the noodles and another thirty minutes to make the sauce."

Taking the towel from him, Diana dried her hands. "Even if the fettuccine hadn't turned out right, we would have been so hungry, we would have eaten it anyway."

Michael looked down at her. Somewhere between kneading the dough and cutting it into strips with the machine, she had removed her shoes. Her sleeves were rolled up to her elbows and a towel matching his was tied around her waist. He couldn't think of any other woman he knew who was so natural and comfortable to be with. Comfortable? What an odd word to spring into his mind. The fire she ignited in his body certainly wasn't comfortable.

He stroked her cheek, startling her.

"You have some flour on your face."

His touch sent a curious current of heat over her skin. She raised her hand and lightly brushed the firm line of his jaw. "So do you."

His gaze moved down the front of her dress, and his hand followed. He heard her sharp intake of breath as his fingers made contact with the gentle slope of her breast.

She glanced down. Her pulse quickened. Swallowing

with difficulty, she brought her eyes back to his. "There's no flour on my dress."

A corner of his mouth lifted into a sensual smile. "I know."

After a short pause she murmured, "Do you usually carry out seduction scenes in the kitchen?"

"You're the only woman who has ever been in my kitchen, other than the lady who comes in twice a week to clean."

Diana didn't want to think about the room he would usually choose to entertain women in. His bedroom.

His fingers continued to brush lightly across her breasts, his touch scorching her skin through the fabric, making it difficult to breathe normally. "From the looks of your cupboards and refrigerator," she said, attempting to keep her tone light, "you don't spend a great deal of time in here either. Aside from a six-pack of beer, a loaf of bread, and a gigantic jar of peanut butter, the only other food in your kitchen is the things you bought to make the fettuccine."

"You didn't look in the freezer. There's a wide variety of TV dinners and frozen pizzas stuffed inside."

He hadn't removed his hand, but was sliding his fingers gently back and forth across her sensitive breast. Striving for a coolness she was far from feeling, she asked, "Not exactly a gourmet?"

His eyes followed the movement of his hand. "To me a kitchen is like a foreign country. Uncharted territory. I know kitchens are necessary, but about all I use this one for is making coffee and throwing frozen meals into the oven." She wrinkled her nose. "Hey, I can unwrap a TV dinner and shove it in the oven with the best of them."

"That's all you live on? Frozen dinners?"

"Don't forget the peanut butter."

"Michael, you should eat decent meals."

His hand traveled from her breasts up her neck to just under her chin. Her eyes were waiting for his when he finally raised his gaze to lock with hers.

"You sound like my mother," he said. "I don't want you to feel maternal toward me, Diana. I want you to feel a lot of things, but maternal isn't one of them."

Lowering his head, he claimed her mouth in a seductive kiss. His lips tasted and teased as his arms brought her into the cradle of his hips. He leaned back against the counter, pulling her with him.

After an initial hesitation, Diana gave in to the need coiling through her. She was off balance in more ways than one as she pressed into his warm, hard body, her mouth opening under the subtle pressure of his hunger. Her hands felt the muscles of his arms as she held on for dear life under the sensual onslaught of rioting emotions.

"Diana," he breathed as he finally broke away from her mouth and let his lips forage at her neck. His arms held her trembling body against his as he tried to control the desire searing through him like a raging fire. He had only meant to kiss her, to test her reaction. His own reaction stunned him.

She pushed away from him enough to see his face. "Michael . . ." she began hesitantly, not sure what she wanted to say.

His hands released their tight hold on her and rested on the soft curve of her hips. "It's all right. I don't plan on ravishing you among the fettuccine makings." He took a long, deep breath. "I'm not as clever as I thought I was."

She had no idea what he meant, but she wasn't going to ask him to clarify his words. Things were moving fast enough between them as it was.

"How clever are you at making coffee?" she asked.

He smiled, accepting her withdrawal. "I'm brilliant."

Reluctantly he let go of her and turned to look for the coffeepot. His hand was shaking as he poured coffee grounds into the basket. He felt as nervous and anxious as when he'd fumbled his way through a crush on the girl next door when he was fourteen. You aren't fourteen now, he told himself as he measured the water. Another thought came into his head. You're in deep trouble, Michael Dare. Deep, serious trouble.

Even without an elaborate coffee maker like Diana's, he managed to prepare a pot of steaming coffee. By the time Diana had finished cleaning off the table, the coffee was ready.

Getting a tray from a cupboard, he said, "Let's have the coffee in the living room. I never want to see this kitchen again."

He was carrying the tray, containing the pot of coffee and cups into the living room, when the doorbell rang. He set the tray on a large, round coffee table and went to the door. When he came back, Diana, sitting on the couch, was surprised to see that he had company.

She was a tiny, frail woman in her seventies, dressed in a prim navy blue dress with a dainty lace collar and white trim down the rather flat front. She barely reached Michael's chest, but she moved with nervous energy, like an elderly hummingbird. She was carrying a plate covered with a spotless white cloth.

If Michael was irritated by the interruption, he certainly didn't let on in front of the woman, whom he introduced as Mrs. Agatha Witherspoon, his neighbor from across the hall. He got another cup from the kitchen, and Mrs. Witherspoon pulled the cloth off the plate to reveal succulent apple turnovers. Their aroma filled every corner of the room. Then, smiling timidly, Mrs. Witherspoon perched on the couch next to Diana.

In one breath she apologized sweetly for bothering them and with the next began an incredible saga of being followed by a potential mugger. It was a colorful, imaginative tale about how a man had followed her from the bank to the grocery store and the clever way she had lost him on the way back to her apartment.

Michael listened patiently, letting her tell her story without interruption and finally reassuring her that four locks on her door should be enough to keep out any intruder. This was a regular occurrence between him and his elderly neighbor. A little chat over freshly baked confections, the latest episode of Mrs. Witherspoon and a suspected rapist/mugger/thief/burglar. Then he would praise her for escaping yet another potentially dangerous individual and advise her to lock her door.

The ritual out of the way, Mrs. Witherspoon pressed the apple turnovers on Michael and Diana, not satisfied until they had eaten two. She asked Diana a variety of questions about where she lived, what she did for a living, and how she had met Michael.

When she learned about the incident in the courtroom, she exclaimed to Diana, "How brave of you! I must remember that. I never thought of using a shoe against an attacker!" Then she scolded Michael. "But a ladies' rest room? Really, Michael. I would think you could have found a more romantic place to meet Miss Dragas."

He grinned. "It was either that or the broom closet."

Finally, with a promise to bring Michael his favorite chocolate brownies the next day, Mrs. Witherspoon said good-bye, picked up her empty plate, and was ready to return to her locked vault across the hall.

While Michael walked Mrs. Witherspoon to her apartment, Diana looked around the living room. One wall consisted of a shelf unit containing an astounding array of technical equipment. Some pieces she recognized, but she hadn't the faintest idea what some other pieces were or what they did. It seemed she and Michael had something in common. Gadgets. Except his gadgets were more sophisticated than her small appliances.

The rest of the room could have passed as a layout for an ad for the perfect apartment. Everything was in place—not a speck of dust, earth tones, tan carpet, brown sofa and chairs and matching brown drapes—and completely impersonal. There were no personal photographs, not a single magazine or book. It could have been anyone's living room.

What a contradiction he was, she thought. Kind to little old ladies. Subsisting on frozen dinners. Driving a classic car. Living in an expensive apartment that resembled a hotel room. Devastatingly sure of himself, and too sexy for his own good . . . or hers.

Michael came back into the room. He poured himself another cup of coffee and sank down next to Diana on the sofa, propping his feet up on the coffee table. It was odd how right it felt for her to be here beside him, he mused. The apartment took on a completely different atmosphere, more comfortable, more of a home, rather than merely somewhere to keep his clothes and collect his mail.

"Michael?"

He turned his head to look at her. "What?"

"Does Mrs. Witherspoon often run into so many bad guys?"

"Only in her imagination. The muggers aren't real, but her fears are. She was attacked several years ago. She wasn't hurt, but her Social Security check was stolen. Now she sees a potential mugger whenever she goes out on the street."

"It must be terrible to live in fear like that."

He smiled. "I think she secretly enjoys the drama it brings to her otherwise quiet life. It's the highlight of her day to tell me about her close calls, real or imaginary. She's very lonely."

"It's nice of you to take the time to listen to her. Not many people would."

"You would."

Diana looked startled at the certainty in his voice. "I would? Do you think you know me that well?"

His eyes glinted with a strange light. "Yes, I think I do." He changed the subject. "Now I know how directors of live television feel."

His disgusted tone made her laugh. "Why?"

"This evening hasn't exactly followed the original script."

Her eyes widened in astonishment. "You made up a script for tonight?" She didn't know whether to be furious or to burst out laughing.

He stretched out his legs and crossed one ankle over the other, perfectly relaxed and at ease. "Only in my head. I tend to be very methodical about things. I'm a compulsive list-maker. I wasn't going to leave anything to chance tonight. It was going to be a perfect evening, with a perfect dinner, perfect wine, all to impress you with how clever I am."

"It has been a perfect evening. The fettuccine was delicious. You may have noticed I had seconds."

He smiled. "That's because you were starving."

"The evening may not have followed your script, but I've enjoyed it."

"It's been different." He shifted sideways to face her, bending one leg under him. His arm lay across the back of the sofa, his hand tantalizingly close to her shoulder, and his leg pressed against her thigh.

"We haven't gone completely through the script yet," he said softly.

Her breath caught in her throat. "Really? What's left?"

"The finale." His fingers played with several strands of her hair. "I've changed the ending I had planned, though. The original script called for delivering you to your floating house at a reasonable hour, with a chaste kiss on your charming mouth."

She ran her tongue over her dry lips. "And now?"

His eyes followed the movement of her tongue. He wanted to feel it stroke his mouth, his skin. He shifted as his slacks grew uncomfortably tight.

"Now I want you to stay the night."

He hadn't wrapped his words in flowery phrases or attempted to pressure her with his touch. He let his eyes and his voice do the persuading.

After a long pause she murmured, "I think we should stick to the original script."

He could have put money on her answer. A corner of his mouth lifted in a mocking smile. "You're very good at that."

"At what?"

"At projecting that cool, unflappable front. It makes me wonder what it would take to shake you. Sixteen-year-old boys with guns and students with switchblades don't do it. Invitations to spend the night hardly cause a blink of an eye."

"An invitation?" she asked dryly. "It sounded like a proposition. A little short of snapping your fingers, but still a proposition."

"Well, you see, this is sort of new to me. I usually don't spend this much time talking about taking a woman to bed." His fingers trailed over the delicate line of her throat. "Your pulse is racing. Maybe you aren't as cool as I thought."

Cool? She was burning up.

As his hand trailed down to her breast, he felt her tremble. "I could make you want me."

It hadn't been a question, but she answered anyway. "Yes."

His thumb stroked the hard, responsive tip of her breast, and tingling pleasure shot through her. "You're halfway there already. Why don't you admit you would like to stay the night?"

"I would like to stay."

His eyes blazed in triumph, and he began to lean toward her, but then she spoke again.

"But I'm not going to."

Instead of demanding to know why, he accepted her refusal. Smiling down at her, he said, "It's enough you want to . . . for now. Come on, I'll take you home."

The part about the chaste kiss at her door was changed slightly as he took her in his arms and kissed her long and hungrily. She was momentarily stunned by the strength of his passion, and grateful that he had so graciously accepted her decision about the end of their evening.

Lifting his head, he asked, "Tomorrow night?"

"There's the party at Rena and Abe's."

"I know. I've been invited, too, remember?"

"You still want to see me after . . . Well, the evening didn't . . . I mean I didn't . . ."

He chuckled. "Did you expect me to pout because we didn't make love?"

"Maybe sulk a little. Some men do."

He lowered his head and brushed her lips with his. "When are you going to realize I'm not like most men?"

She ran her tongue over her lips, savoring the taste of him. "I think I already know that."

"Good Lord, Diana. Don't do that."

"What? I'm only answering your question."

"It's not what you said. It's what you did. Do you have any idea what it does to me to see that pink tongue stroking your flesh? Someday, moon goddess, I'm going to feel it on mine. See you tomorrow night."

Diana watched him walk away, her body suddenly trembling. She opened her mouth to call him back, but no sound came out. She had done the right thing by refusing to go to bed with him. Her mind knew that. It was too bad her body couldn't agree.

Four

The wide neckline of her oversized sweat shirt fell over Diana's bare shoulder as she knelt down to reach under the dresser in her bedroom. It wasn't there. She stood up, placing her hands on her jean-clad hips, and looked around the room. On her right foot was a soft white leather moccasin. She was searching for the left one.

There was one place she hadn't looked, and that was under the bed. Lying on her stomach, she crawled under the queen-sized bed and swept her arm across the floor. Nothing. Wiggling her hips, she inched farther under the bed, until only her hips and legs were visible.

Using less-than-ladylike language when she bumped against the hard bed spring, she wasn't aware of the sound of footsteps approaching the bedroom. Her fingers finally closed around the missing moccasin.

A masculine voice spoke somewhere above her. "Did the houseboat spring a leak?"

Diana froze. Then she twisted her head to look in the direction of the voice. She saw a pair of brown loafers parked next to her legs. The shoes moved and jean-covered knees took their place. Then a man's head and shoulders came into view.

"Michael!"

His attention was diverted by her squirming, wig-

gling bottom as she began to crawl backward. The fa(
that she was wearing only one shoe didn't hold h
interest as much as the sight of her legs and hip
gyrating provocatively on the floor.

Her voice sounded muffled and slightly strangle(
"What are you doing here?"

"I don't remember," he said absently as he watche(
her contortions.

She yelped and stopped moving. He peered under th(
bed. "What's wrong?"

"My hair is caught on something."

It took him only a second to join her under the be(
his shoulders brushing hers. It took another minut
for him to assess the situation and remove the lock (
her hair caught on a splinter of wood on the bed frame

Once she was free, she turned her head to look a
him. He grinned and said, "Hi."

His face was only inches from hers. Diana's breath
caught as she inhaled his male scent and felt the hea(
emanating from his body, sprawled so close to hers.

Her reply came out huskier than she would hav(
liked. "Hi." Forcing her mind to concentrate on he
original question, she asked, "Why are you here?"

"I'm getting you untangled from your bed."

"I mean why are you here this morning? The part\
isn't until tonight."

It was a good question, a natural question, h(
thought. It was also one he didn't have a sane answe\
for. He could tell her how he'd needed to hear her velve\
voice when he woke up that morning. How he'd ache(
to touch her silky skin and had wanted to see her, ha(
to see her in the flesh, and not in his mind. He opte(
for a vague reply.

"I saw your pennant, so I knew you were home."

She gave him a skeptical glance. "You just happened
to be in the neighborhood?"

"Something like that."

The neckline of her loose-fitting top was slowly sliding down to expose a golden shoulder only a breath away from his mouth. The fragrance of her skin beckoned, and he wasn't strong enough to resist.

When his warm lips touched her shoulder, she jerked in surprise, bumping her head on the box springs. "Ouch! That hurt!"

"I only kissed your shoulder. How can you say that hurt?"

"I bumped my head, you idiot."

His deep chuckle vibrated in the closed-in space under the bed. "Then you shouldn't have pulled away. It was only a kiss. You're in no danger of having your gorgeous body ravished, under the circumstances. I do much better on top of a bed than under it."

Diana didn't doubt his claim one bit. "I didn't know it was you. I thought it was a spider."

He made an odd, choking sound. "A spider? Thanks a whole bunch."

"Don't get your macho ego all bent out of shape. I wasn't expecting you to kiss any part of me."

"Well, let me give you advance warning." He cupped the back of her neck. "This is me, not some creepy, crawly insect, so don't do anything dumb like trying to get away."

His mouth closed over hers in a fierce kiss, establishing his claim. Diana closed her eyes as shafts of heat jolted through her. Even if she had wanted to—which she didn't—it would have been physically impossible to move away. There wasn't enough space under the bed for her to move closer to his hard body, either, but she did open her mouth under his, responding to his sensual demands.

Forgetting for a moment where they were, Michael began to turn in order to feel her slender body along his aching length, but had to stop when his elbow came in contact with the bed. Reluctantly dragging his mouth from hers, he murmured, "Do you think we could continue this somewhere else other than under your bed? I'm getting a kink in my neck."

Still holding on to the moccasin. Diana scooted out from under the bed and stood up. What in the world had come over her? she asked herself. She had been kissing him under her bed! She quickly put the moccasin on while Michael got to his feet. Dressed in jeans and a light blue shirt, with the sleeves rolled up to his elbows, he looked lean and masculine and perfectly at ease in her bedroom.

His dark eyes locked with hers, and she saw the smoldering light in their depths.

Deciding her bedroom wasn't a practical place to stay under the circumstances, she headed for the living area. Since he hadn't answered her question about why he was there the two times she had asked it, she figured she'd give it one more try. It was a safer subject than talking about what had just happened under her bed.

"You still haven't told me why you happen to be in Sausalito at nine in the morning. Or, to be more exact, why you were in my bedroom at—" Her hands clamped down on her hips as something else occurred to her. "You walked right in as if you owned the place. Haven't you ever heard of ringing the doorbell?"

He couldn't help smiling. It had taken her a while to figure that out. "You don't have one to ring."

"Yes, I do. It's a cowbell hanging by the door. You pull the string and it goes clang."

A bell by the door. A doorbell. Of course. "I didn't see it. I knocked but you didn't respond."

"So you walked right into my bedroom."

"Diana, one advantage of the wide-open layout of your home is that it takes only a second to glance around to determine if the room is occupied or unoccupied. When I didn't see you in the kitchen or living room, I made the brilliant deduction you must be in either the bedroom or the bathroom. One peek behind the screen revealed two legs and a rather charming rear end sticking out from under a bed. I didn't have to look in the bathroom. You were under the bed. Wearing only one shoe but definitely under the bed."

"I was looking for the other moccasin."

"I figured that out when I saw it in your hand. So what do you want to do today?"

She tilted her head to one side as she studied him, noting the confident gleam in his eyes. The blasted man arrived unannounced, walked into her home as if he owned the place, and took it for granted she would automatically be thrilled to spend the day with him. Well, hold on to your socks, hotshot, she thought. You can't have everything your way. She refused to acknowledge the pleasure she felt that he *had* sought her out this morning.

"I have some errands to take care of," she said.

"I'll drive you wherever you have to go."

"I have a *lot* of errands to run this morning," she said emphatically, picking up a list off the table and waving it in the air.

"Then we'd better get going."

Well, she had tried. If he was bored out of his mind, he couldn't say he hadn't been warned. She had given him a choice and he had made it.

The first stop they made was the dry cleaner's, where Diana picked up two suits and three pairs of slacks. Michael gallantly offered to carry them, thinking they would be going back to the car. Diana began walking in the opposite direction, though. He hoisted the plastic-wrapped clothing over his shoulder by the wire hangers and followed her. She stopped at a drugstore to purchase shampoo and several other items, and gave him the bag to carry.

When they left the drugstore she was hailed by a bearded man wearing wrinkled jeans a size too big for his thin frame. His faded denim work shirt, designed for a man thirty pounds heavier, looked as though it were draped on a misshapen clothes hanger. Diana introduced him as Dale. He gave Michael only a slight nod of acknowledgment before returning his attention to Diana and asking her a question that caused Michael to blink in astonishment. As they talked, Michael shifted the loads he was carrying from one hand to the other. The wire hangers holding Diana's clothes had been digging into his palm. A few minutes later Dale resumed his quick, nervous gait, moving away from them, and Michael turned to Diana.

"Did that guy just ask you if your ficus was happy?"

Stopping to peer in a store window, she said, "Yes, he did. Look at this piece of stoneware, Michael. The one that looks like a wizard holding a crystal ball. He's frowning and scratching his head as though he can't make head or tail out of something."

Michael knew how the guy felt. "About the happy ficus. What or who is a ficus?"

Diana tore her gaze away from the window and smiled at his bewildered expression. "It's the small leafy tree on one side of my bay window. I bought it from Dale's nursery, and he wanted to know how it was doing. That reminds me, I need to get plant food."

The plant food was purchased after they had popped into several other places, one being a gallery where she had taken a painting to be framed. She showed the painting to Michael, explaining that her friend, Nicole, was the artist and that she was having an exhibit in San Francisco in November. Michael noticed the many people who stopped to talk to Diana throughout the morning, several asking if she would be at the Piccolos' party that evening. He recognized some of the people. One was a stage actor and another a well-known jazz pianist currently residing in Sausalito. In one store a middle-aged man cornered Michael and told him how much he had enjoyed the documentary on homeless people, but generally the people they talked to were acquaintances of Diana's.

Eventually, Michael's arms became cramped from carrying the growing load of merchandise, and he insisted they return to the car to drop everything off.

Diana was surprised by Michael's attitude. She had expected him to be fed up with trailing after her, but he actually seemed to be enjoying himself. When they met another couple she knew, as they were walking back to the car, Michael joked about not being able to shake hands because of her penchant for buying up half of downtown Sausalito.

Another hour, broken up by a second trip to the car with packages, went by before she finally checked off the last item on her list and announced, "Lunch."

The restaurant was small and packed with people. While they waited in line, Diana chatted with a few people she knew, introducing them to Michael. Finally they were shown to a table. While Diana studied the menu, Michael studied her. After spending the morning with her, he was no closer to finding a niche to fit her into. Usually he could come up with a certain phrase to describe someone, but she defied any one category. She was a multi-faceted individual with such hidden depths, and he hadn't even begun to scratch the surface.

It didn't matter who she spoke to—the snooty gallery owner, the gray-haired dowager swimming in pearls, the elderly shoe repairman—everyone was treated the same way, with a reserved friendliness. She allowed people to come only so close to the invisible boundary she had erected around herself.

She looked up and caught his intent gaze on her. "Have you made up your mind?" she asked.

Was his expression that easy to read? he wondered. He didn't think his confusion showed. "Not yet."

"It would be easier to choose if you read the menu," she said dryly, glancing at the unopened menu in front of him.

"I wonder if they have humble pie," he said as he opened the menu.

She blinked. "Humble pie?"

"Isn't that what I should be eating? Or am I wrong in

assuming my role as bag boy this morning was punishment for arriving unannounced and insisting you spend the day with me without asking first?"

"I had things to do, and they had to get done. If you had asked what my plans were, I would have told you about all the chasing around I had to do. I did try to warn you, if you remember."

He looked at her sharply. "You also could have told me to get lost. Why didn't you?"

Apparently, beating around the bush wasn't his style, she thought. Well, it wasn't hers either. "Curiosity."

His smile was pained. "You're rather hard on a man's ego, Diana. Here I was hoping I was irresistible and you wanted my company. What were you curious about? How many packages I could tote before collapsing?"

The waiter approached the table then, and Diana gave him her order. Michael echoed it, not particularly caring what he ate, and impatient to hear her answer to his question.

When she didn't immediately speak after the waiter left, he prodded. "Well?"

"Well, what?"

Michael mentally counted to ten. "You said you were curious about me. Why not just ask me whatever it is you want to know?"

"Anyone can ask questions. That shows no imagination. I found out more by doing it my way."

His mind flashed back to their morning together, going over the things they had talked about, the places they had gone. Not a clue. "You're going to have to help me, Diana. What did you find out?"

Leaning back in her chair, she gazed directly at him. "You are patient, flexible but not a pushover, and you like children."

"Really? May I ask how you figured all that out?"

"You're patient and good-natured even when you don't get your own way. I'm sure following me around Sausalito has not been the highlight of your week. You can be pushed only so far and then you put your foot down, like when you insisted on going back to the car to dump an armload of packages. You like people, especially children, even when that little boy dropped his chocolate ice cream cone on your foot. You even gave him money to buy another one, instead of getting angry."

She smiled at the waiter as he set her lunch in front of her, missing the stunned look on Michael's face. "This looks good. I'm starving."

The waiter set a plate in front of Michael. "Will there be anything else, sir?"

"What? No, nothing, thank you." Michael was too busy absorbing what Diana had just told him to think about anything as mundane as food. It was a new experience to be analyzed and dissected. It made him feel oddly exposed . . . and irritated that she could read him so easily and he couldn't read her at all. No, he thought, that wasn't entirely true. He could read her up to a point, but some of the pages of her life were missing. Hell, whole chapters were missing. All he had to do was use his head instead of his loins when he was around her.

She took the first bite of her meal. Suddenly she exploded. "I don't believe it. I don't bloody believe it."

He looked on in astonishment as she shoved her chair back and stormed off toward a swinging door at the back of the restaurant. Resigned to his fate, he sighed and followed her. She was leading him a merry chase in more ways than one.

The door swung open as a waiter carrying a tray shoved it from the other side. He gave Michael a sidelong glance, then continued on his way. Michael caught the door before it had a chance to close, and entered, stopping just inside.

Diana was standing in front of a large man dressed all in white, with a starched scarf tied in sailor's knot about his neck. He was on the receiving end of a blistering chewing-out in what sounded, literally, like Greek to Michael. The cook didn't attempt to defend himself until Diana ran down. His defense was soft-spoken and brief, but effective. Mollified, Diana left the kitchen.

Michael held the door open for her. "What was that all about?" he asked as she brushed by him.

She didn't answer until she was again seated at their table. She took a deep, calming breath, and said, "After badgering me for my grandmother's recipe for moussaka, the blasted man didn't even follow it. He substituted potatoes for eggplant."

"Unforgivable."

"My grandmother would have his ears."

"Understandable."

His tolerant tone filtered through her anger, and she smiled. "You think I'm making a big fuss over such a small thing."

He shook his head. "Your reaction is the same kind I would have if someone misquoted something I wrote or said." He grinned. "You have a more colorful way of protesting. Remind me never to make you mad."

She grinned in return. "We might as well eat his imitation moussaka. I have one more stop to make, and then I need to get back to fix a couple of dishes for the party tonight."

Tucking into the illegitimate dish on his plate, he said, "The Piccolos' party appears to be the social event of the year."

"Month. Rena lives to entertain and Abe loves crowds. Unfortunately, Rena is not at her best in the kitchen, so I help fix a few hors d'oeuvres."

"Tell me about some of the people who will be there."

When she didn't answer right away, he looked up at her. There was a distinct hint of frost in the air. She had put down her fork and was glaring at him with accusing eyes.

"What's wrong?"

"Why do you want to know about the people who will be at the party?"

He hated the suspicion he heard in her voice. "I'm getting a little tired of having to defend every question I ask, Diana. A few of the people who stopped to talk to you this morning discussed the party. Why can't I?" He leaned forward and said bluntly, "I m going to the party as your lover, not as a journalist."

She gasped. "You're not my lover," she said heatedly.

"Not yet, but I will be."

Indignation, anger, stupefaction, and excitement all vied for position within her. She opened her mouth, but clamped it shut when something caught her eye. She quickly bent over as if to pick something up off the floor as a flash of light exploded around their table.

Turning toward the source of the light, Michael saw an attractive blond with a camera. It wasn't a small tourist's camera, but one better suited to a journalist.

The blonde walked over to the table. "Diana Dragas, you rat. You ruined my picture."

Diana straightened up in her chair once she saw the camera was no longer aimed in her direction. "I'm going to ruin more than that, Zelda, if you point that thing at me again."

"Be fair," Zelda protested. "I heard you had latched on to Michael Dare, so I wanted a few pictures for the paper."

"Take his picture then. You don't need me in it."

"Local color," Zelda drawled. She turned to Michael. "You don't mind if I take your picture, do you, Mr. Dare? A girl has to make a living."

Diana ground her teeth when she saw the smile Michael sent in Zelda's direction. It could have melted the ice cap.

"Of course I don't mind," he said, "but why waste your film on me?" He went on to tell her that he'd seen a popular local singer down on the waterfront with a young lady dressed in a skimpy pink outfit.

Zelda's green eyes glittered like a Fourth of July sparkler. Without further delay she left the restaurant. Obviously, there was nothing more tempting than the possibility of a naughty rendezvous, especially compared to a boring, respectable lunch.

Michael dug money out of his pocket and tossed it onto the table. Standing up, he grabbed Diana's hand and pulled her out of her chair. As he hustled her outside and headed toward his car, she asked, "What's the rush?"

"I don't want your friend Zelda coming back to look for us." He grinned. "She's not going to be fond of me."

"Why?"

"The girl in the skimpy pink outfit is Mitch's two-year-old daughter."

Diana laughed as they reached the car and he unlocked her door. "Zelda will be furious. I thought you journalists stuck together. You just sent her off on a wild-goose chase."

Michael wasn't smiling as he got in the driver's seat and started the engine. "Zealous Zelda is not a journalist. She's the type who checks only her own name for accuracy when it's printed under a headline. Let's forget about her. You said you have another stop to make."

She gave him directions to the grocery store, and wasn't surprised when he came in with her rather than staying in the car. He pushed the cart up and down the aisles, occasionally grabbing an item that caught his eye.

"Put those marshmallows back, Michael."

"Why? Do you have some at home?"

"No."

"Then they stay."

"Michael, look at this list."

"I'm looking at it."

"Do you see pretzels written anywhere?"

"No."

"Then why did you just put a bag of pretzels in the cart?"

"To go with the beer."

"What beer?"

"The beer under the bag of pretzels."

It took several trips to unload everything from Michael's car. He offered to help make the hors d'oeuvres, but Diana shoved a beer and the bag of pretzels at him and ordered him out of the kitchen. They chatted companionably as she worked, until he announced that he had to return to his apartment in San Francisco to change for the party.

To Diana, her home seemed oddly empty after he had gone. She put on a record to chase away the silence and forced herself to concentrate on her cooking. She should be glad he had left. The man was bonkers. Totally round the bend. He had told her he was going to the party as her lover as though it were a predetermined fact of life. He was taking a lot for granted again, taking her for granted.

Just because she had responded slightly when he kissed her . . . Slightly? Who was she trying to kid? Evidently herself. She doubted if she had fooled Michael one bit.

As a result of an accident on the Golden Gate Bridge, Michael arrived back at Diana's a little before seven, later than he had planned. Even though he hadn't asked her, he had wanted to take her out to dinner. Maybe this time they would actually eat the whole meal. So far they hadn't done too well in restaurants.

He rang the cowbell several times, not making the mistake of knocking. She didn't come to the door, but he heard a sound that he interpreted as "come in," and opened the door.

He immediately saw her standing at the kitchen counter with her back to him. She was wearing a short, kimono-style robe that bared a generous expanse of tanned legs. Her hair was pulled up on top of her head, and several ebony strands, damp from her recent shower, clung to her neck. She was holding a towel to her face, wiping her eyes.

She was crying!

He rushed over to her and spun her around. "Why are you crying? Did you cut yourself?"

She made an inarticulate sound and dabbed at her eyes. He pulled her into his arms. The sight of her tears was ripping him to shreds.

"Diana, honey, what's wrong? Tell me what's wrong."

An inelegant sniffle accompanied a muffled, "Nothing's wrong." Diana felt like an absolute idiot, but she couldn't stop the tears from cascading down her cheeks.

He pleaded with her. "Diana, please don't cry. I can't stand it."

His hands soothed her with gentle strokes across her back as he held her against his hard body. He kissed her forehead, eyes, neck, cheeks, and finally her mouth. He could taste her salty tears on his tongue.

As much as she was enjoying his kisses, she knew he deserved an explanation. "Michael, I'm all right. I was peeling onions."

His mouth, his hands, his entire body became still. Then his shoulders shook slightly and she heard a stifled sound of amusement. He pressed a brief kiss on her neck before he raised his head.

Golden lights of humor flickered in his sable eyes as he looked down at her. "What's the Greek word for trouble?"

She told him.

He tried it, coming very close to pronouncing it correctly. "It should be your middle name. It fits."

"Thank you very much," she said with mock indignation.

"You're welcome."

His hands were on the move again, leaving a tingling trail of sensation in their wake. She placed her own hands on his chest and said, "Michael, I have to get dressed. The party. Remember?"

"In a minute. I was ready to comfort you when I thought you were crying. Now it's your turn to comfort me. Finding you in tears has been a traumatic experience."

"How about a cup of tea? It's supposed to work wonders for all sorts of ailments and traumas. My mother swears by it."

"I'd rather have you."

He lowered his head. His hands cupped her buttocks to bring her into the cradle of his hips as his mouth closed over her parted lips. The shattering explosion he felt inside was becoming familiar, and impossible to live without. Only Diana could make his body, his mind, his temperature soar instantly.

It was a good thing Michael was holding her, Diana thought. Her legs trembled as his mouth moved over hers and his tongue plunged inside. She gripped the lapels of his sport coat. She was drowning in a whirlpool of delicious sensations, and he was her only lifeline.

He slowly lowered her to the floor, until she was standing on her own. His hands slipped into the opening of her robe, sliding across her rib cage and up to her bare breasts.

She gasped. Her body shuddered. Her flesh seemed so cold except where he was touching her, sending flames of red-hot desire over her skin.

He sank against the edge of the table, half-sitting as he pulled her between his thighs. A fierce exultation surged through him when he felt the thrust of her nipples against his palms. Her response was everything he could have hoped for, and it certainly didn't help control the hot rush of need soaring through his veins.

Diana's heart was thudding madly in her chest. Trapped between his hard thighs, she arched her body into his, feeling him shudder against her.

"You feel so good, Diana," he said hoarsely against her neck. "So soft, so exciting, so desirable."

"Michael, no." Was that her voice? That husky, throaty sound?

"Why turn me down when I haven't asked you for anything yet?"

"Haven't you?"

He raised his head, and his eyes searched hers as his hands slid down to her bare waist. "Maybe I have. I want you very badly, and I can't hide that. From the way you respond to me, I get the impression you want me too. But you like to be in control, don't you, Diana, and you can't control my reaction to you or your reaction to me. That's why you're saying no, isn't it?"

"No."

He scowled at her. "I'm developing a strong dislike for that particular word. Could you possibly be a little more explicit?"

She took a steadying breath. It was time to jump off the fence, on one side or the other. "I like you to touch me, to hold me. When you kiss me, I want more. I want *you*, but if we go any further now, we'll end up in my bedroom for a long time. If I don't appear next door, Rena will come looking for me. That's why I said no."

He smiled with satisfaction. She wasn't refusing his lovemaking, only postponing it. He removed his hands from her tempting flesh and smoothed her robe back into place.

"All right," he said. "I promise not to throw you down on the table and have my way with you. Let's go to that damned party."

She gazed steadily at him, allowing him to see the passion in her eyes. Passion for him. Her hands rested lightly on his chest, and she could feel the heavy beat of his heart. "Am I messing up your script for a torrid love scene?"

He shook his head. "What will happen isn't just up to me." His smile was a little off-center. "You have an important part in any love scene involving us, you know. Without you, I would have a difficult time getting through any seduction scene. In fact, I would look pretty ridiculous."

Diana smiled. She couldn't help it. He made her smile at the damnedest things at the damnedest time. Her body was still throbbing with desire, and she could feel his arousal still pressing against her. His blood hadn't cooled either. Yet he could make her smile.

He released her reluctantly and retied the sash around her slim waist. "Is this what you plan to wear to the party tonight? If so, may I suggest several strands of barbed wire around this sash and a 'Keep Off' sign? It comes untied awfully easily, and I would hate to have to bash some guy's nose in if someone other than me has his hands on it."

"I have a quite-respectable frock to wear, so the barbed wire won't be necessary."

"Glad to hear it." He still held on to the ends of the sash. With a slight tug on them, he brought her forward so he could give her a short, hard kiss. "Need any help with your . . . ah, frock?"

"I can manage, thank you."

"I was afraid you were going to say that."

Five

The Piccolos' party was a treasure trove of celebrities, neighbors, and business people. Among them were a couple of local politicians, a minister, several lawyers, a golf pro, some artists, a schoolteacher, a few musicians, and no reporters. Technically Michael could be classed as one, but he appeared to be off duty.

He quickly made it clear who he was with and why. He stayed as close to Diana as a limpet to a rock. There were numerous opportunities for him to make valuable contacts, especially for the program he and his staff were researching, but he wasn't there for business reasons. Not once did he bring up his work or inquire about anyone else's.

Diana didn't need to introduce him to most of the guests. They knew who he was. He was often asked what he was working on now, but he fielded the questions adroitly. He knew Diana still wasn't comfortable with his occupation, and he wasn't about to confirm her theory about grasping journalists. The only thing he wanted to grasp that evening was her.

When Diana realized Michael was not making any journalistic noises, she began to relax and enjoy the evening with him. If he could forget he was a journalist, so could she.

She gave him a tour of the Piccolos' houseboat, which was completely the opposite of hers. Where the builder of her houseboat preferred space, the one who had constructed the Piccolos' must have had a fondness for rabbit hutches. After she had led Michael through the maze of rooms and the crush of people, she asked him which room he wanted to return to. "As you can see, there's something to suit everyone. You can play bridge, eat, see a home movie, dance, play games, or grab a musical instrument and join the band."

"Is it always like this?" he asked, standing close to her so she could hear him over the hum and buzz of conversation surrounding them.

"Sometimes there are more people. Sometimes fewer. Occasionally, when some of the usual guests are on vacation or out of town, you can actually take two steps without bumping into someone."

"I meant, are there usually so many activities for people to do? It's like a cruise ship with a hyperactive social director."

She laughed. "I suppose it does seem odd if you aren't used to it. You may have noticed there's no alcohol served here except Rena's fruit punch, which could take paint off a chair. Only a few rugged individuals with cast-iron constitutions go back to the punch bowl for seconds. To give everyone something to do other than get plastered, Rena started setting out games for people to play. Then one night they showed home movies and someone volunteered to bring his collection of vacation films. Another night one of the musicians brought his guitar. You get the idea."

He nodded. "What if someone just wants to talk without having to yell or read lips?"

"There is Abe's study or the solarium." She paused thoughtfully "No. There will be a chess match going on in the study, and I saw several women heading toward the solarium."

She hesitated again, then looked directly at him. "Is finding someplace quiet important to you?"

He smiled slowly, his dark gaze flowing over her face. "Oh, yes."

"Well, I guess there's only one place left. The crow's nest."

"Lead the way."

The way was up the stairs, out the second-story window of Nicole's old bedroom, and up a wooden ladder attached to the outside of the house, to a flat section of roof. There was a waist-high wooden rail around the small area, creating a widow's walk. The view was spectacular, with the lights of Sausalito on one side and the dark outline of Angel Island visible in the moonlight. The night was cool and windy, so that even though the roof might not have been the most comfortable place to be, it was private and quiet.

The strong breeze caught Diana's hair and the thin material of her dress as she stood near the rail and looked out at the bay over the top of several other houseboats. The moonlight subtly lit her face and picked up silver highlights in her ebony hair. She looked elemental, vital, and so excitingly feminine, she took his breath away.

She wrapped her arms around her waist, and he moved to stand directly behind her. He slipped his arms around her under her breasts, surrounding her with the protection of his body.

"Is that better?" he asked.

Her hands rested on his arms, and she leaned her head back against his shoulder. "Hmmm."

"Do you want to go back inside, where it's warmer?"

She shook her head. "It's quiet here. Nicole and I used to sneak up here to get away from the noise and the crowds. Sometimes we brought food and had our own party. I think Rena knew where we had disappeared to, but she never said anything."

"Don't you like these parties?"

"I used to be one of the last ones to leave when I first moved here. Everyone was so uninhibited, so free. Rena's parties were exciting, and so different from the more formal atmosphere I was brought up in. Somehow it isn't the same since Nicole was in that accident and left to hibernate in the mountains."

"You prefer beer and pretzels to tea and crumpets?"

"As a change, but not necessarily a steady diet."

"You like change, don't you, Diana? Different places, unusual situations, interesting people."

There was no censure in his voice. He had simply made a statement based on what he'd learned during their short acquaintance. His assessment was disturbingly accurate.

"Most of my life has consisted of different places, unusual situations, and interesting people."

"Rena told the lady she introduced us to when we first arrived that she had gone to school with your mother. How did that come about? Rena's an American and you said your mother is English."

"They're as different as chalk and cheese, but have been close friends ever since they met in finishing school in Switzerland. I've known Rena and Abe all my life. They used to move around almost as much as my parents did, but somehow the two families managed to visit each other over the years."

He watched the lights of a boat as it slowly made its way over the dark velvet surface of the bay. "So how did you end up in Sausalito?"

"A friend of my father's asked me to come to San Francisco to translate his grandfather's journals from German to English. He didn't trust the post office to deliver them to me in Washington, D.C. His offer came at a perfect time, since I wanted to leave the capital anyway. I stayed with Rena and Abe until the houseboat next door became vacant. By then I was working as an interpreter for the municipal courts, plus translating the journals, so I was able to support myself."

"Why did you want to get out of D.C.?"

"I had just finished college. My parents were making noises about my teaching at one of the local schools, and . . ."

"And you were ready to venture out on your own?"

"Something like that."

His arms tightened around her as he shifted his body slightly. His warm breath flowed over her hair, sending heat spreading along her veins. It was odd how her insides could be like molten lava and yet a chill was running along her skin.

When Michael felt her shiver, he loosened his hold on her and shrugged off his sports jacket. He turned her toward him and wrapped the coat around her, holding it closed in front. His coat swamped her smaller frame, but it was warm from his body heat and held the scent of his male fragrance. Her feet were cold, too—she had kicked her shoes off in Nicole's bedroom in order to climb the ladder—but she didn't want to trade the privacy they had for the crowded party below.

"Michael," she protested. "You'll be cold now."

He pulled her against him. "Then you keep me warm."

She slipped her arms into the sleeves of his coat, then wrapped her arms and the coat around him as far as the coat would go.

"Tell me about your family," she said softly.

He could feel her breasts pressing against his chest, and his voice was husky as he drawled, "Now?"

"Why not?"

"I can think of a few things I'd rather be doing."

She could too. Her pulse quickened. "Tell me. I want to know."

His hands moved over her back, bringing her even closer. "Compared to your roving family, mine will sound like dull sticks."

"Tell me."

Some of her hair blew across his face, but he didn't attempt to remove it. He took a deep breath, inhaling its flowery scent. When he didn't say anything right away, she prompted him. "Michael?"

"Right." He sighed heavily. "My family. I was born and raised in San Francisco. No brothers or sisters. My

uncle you've met in the courtroom. He and my aunt
live near the Presidio. My father moved to Carmel after
my mother died, about ten years ago. He has a medical
practice there. That's the family tree. A very small tree."

"Do you see your father often?"

"Not as often as I should. If he had stayed in San
Francisco, I would have been able to spend more time
with him. His practice doesn't allow him much free
time to travel to visit me in San Francisco or Los
Angeles, but we manage to see each other whenever I
get to Carmel."

"Why Los Angeles? I thought you lived in San Francisco."

He hesitated. He didn't want to bring up his work. "I
do live in San Francisco. My office and research staff
are in San Francisco. Most of the preliminary work is
done out of my office in San Francisco, but the documentaries are produced in L.A."

She made no comment, and he wished he knew what
she was thinking.

He would have been surprised. Instead of thinking
about his work, she was wondering how much time he
spent in San Francisco, and then was slightly irritated
with herself for further wondering how much of that
time he would spend with her.

Neither spoke for several minutes, and Diana slowly
felt a difference in the way Michael was holding her,
like the tide changing from low to high. A tension was
building in his body, and his arms tightened about her
as his hands began to move across her back.

She raised her head. His face was in shadow, and
she wasn't able to see what was in his eyes. She hoped
he couldn't see hers either. There were so many new
emotions churning in her, and she wasn't sure she
was able to hide any of them from him.

His hands cupped her face, and as he stared down at
her she felt his desire with a force as strong as the
current in the ocean. She expected him to kiss her, but

he only said, "We'd better get back to the party." He dropped his hands away from her, though his eyes never left her face.

Looking down so he couldn't see the disappointment in her own eyes, she withdrew her arms from around his waist and began to remove his coat. She didn't trust her voice to speak, even if she could have thought of anything to say.

Following his instincts instead of his common sense, Michael reached out to stop her movements. He found one of her hands, and brought it up to his chest, spreading her fingers out over his heart. "Do you feel that? That's why we're going back inside. That's what just being near you does to me."

Her eyes were wide as she raised them to meet his. His heart was pounding heavily, vibrating against her sensitive palm.

"You're something new in my life, moon goddess." He pressed her hand against his racing heart. "This is new to me. If I kissed you right now, I'm not sure I could stop. I'm not going to make love to you for the first time on a cold balcony, where we could be interrupted by someone wanting us to play Trivial Pursuit."

He was being honest with her, she thought, more honest than she had been with herself. She didn't pretend she didn't know what he was talking about. What she found amazing was that he was experiencing the same drugging passion she felt.

Just then a few drops of rain fell on them, splattering on the wooden planks at their feet. She tilted her head to one side in that special way he was becoming familiar with, and smiled. "Can I have a rain check?"

"Anytime," he said huskily.

He accepted his coat back from her and slipped it on. In Nicole's bedroom, Diana put her shoes back on and took a few minutes to tame the tangle the wind had created in her hair.

It was close and intimate in the bedroom, with the

rain tapping on the window and the light dim. Michael watched her brush her hair in front of the French-provincial vanity, remembering when they'd met. She had brushed her hair then, too. He had wanted her then, too, but not as badly as he did now.

No matter where she was, she seemed perfectly at home. Her years of moving around from place to place, country to country, had obviously instilled in her an ability to fit into wherever she was and make do with whatever she had. He hoped her ability to adapt carried over to include his profession. She might not like the fact that he was a journalist, but she was going to have to accept it . . . and him.

Diana was wondering if her heartbeat would ever be normal again. The ordinary action of brushing her hair soothed her. It also gave her something to do while she thought about the night ahead. She considered what he had said about this thing between them being new. She had never felt this compelling need for a man's touch before. The coil of desire was frightening . . . and exciting . . . and uncontrollable. This primitive desire for a man had never happened to her before, and she was stunned by the strength of it. And the inevitability of it.

Her eyes met his in the mirror, and she saw the reflection of her aroused senses in his dark gaze. A corner of his mouth curved up briefly. Then he went to the door and opened it, standing to one side as he waited for her to precede him.

They returned to the party. Rena gave Diana a knowing look as she and Michael descended the stairs, but tactfully said nothing. She did tell Diana her presence was being requested in the music room.

Diana groaned. "Strauss is back."

Chuckling, Rena nodded. "Afraid so. I'd better warn you. He's out for blood."

"He's liable to get his wish." Lifting her head, Diana rubbed her fingers together. "I haven't played since the last time he was here, and that was three months ago. My callouses have softened."

Rena shrugged. "You had better get in there and warm up. The last I heard, the odds were three to one."

"In whose favor?"

"Yours."

Diana turned to Michael, who was looking from one woman to the other, completely mystified. "I have to do this, Michael. I'll never live it down if I don't."

"Do what?"

"Make a complete and utter fool of myself."

She took his hand and wove a way through the people standing around the buffet table, heading toward a room from which the sound of a strumming guitar could be heard faintly over the sound of chatting groups of people.

For the next hour, Michael sat on a couch in the living room and watched Diana compete in a musical duel, not a duet, with the man named Strauss. When Diana had entered the room, she was given a rousing welcome. A path was made for her through the people seated on the carpeted floor, so she could get to the stool set next to a large, middle-aged man with shoulder-length black hair and a guitar on his lap. A battered black case was propped against the stool. Diana opened it and took out a banjo of questionable age.

The contest consisted of one person's playing excerpts of a melody, then the other's attempting to play the same tune. They accompanied their music with a great many cheeky remarks in broad cockney accents. Strauss had Diana floundering when he played a complicated flamenco number, but Diana got back at him by playing a quick rendition of a bluegrass tune. They finished by playing "Dueling Banjos" together, much to the delight of their audience.

Diana was laughing when she finally slipped off her stool and hugged Strauss. They were surrounded by their appreciative audience, except for one of the listeners. Michael remained on the couch, his gaze never leaving Diana while she was teased and congratulated. He didn't like Strauss's easy familiarity with her. He now had his arm around Diana, keeping her close against his side.

After seeing Diana with the various people she had talked to that morning and this evening at the party, Michael knew she was exceedingly friendly and didn't consider anyone a stranger. He wanted to be more than a friend, but was that all she wanted from him? A little while ago, it had been *his* arms around her, and now she was allowing another man to hold her.

Michael had never settled for second best in his work. He certainly wasn't going to settle for being one of the pack of men around Diana. He didn't want to be her pal. He wanted to be her lover . . . exclusively.

The first indication he had of someone sitting beside him on the couch was when he heard a man ask, "Did you enjoy the concert?"

He turned and smiled faintly at Abe Piccolo. "Is that what it was? It seemed more like a musical jousting match."

Looking elegantly casual in white slacks, a red shirt, and a dashing yellow ascot, Abe chuckled. "In a way, I suppose it is. All in fun, of course."

"Rena said something about a wager."

Abe nodded. "No money is involved. Just a few verbal bets as to which one will top the other. Adds spice. The winner is decided by the audience." The older man gave Michael a measured look. "Speaking of spice, your presence here has added a dash of excitement."

Michael gave him a skeptical look. "I don't know why. I'm rather small potatoes compared to some of the other people here tonight, including you."

"My dear boy, you are with Diana Dragas and you are a journalist. Considering the one usually will have nothing to do with the other, it causes raised eyebrows."

Michael's gaze shifted to Diana for a moment. Her

distaste for his profession was apparently common knowledge. He couldn't help wondering if he was the only one who didn't know the reason for it. He could ask Abe, but for some strange reason, he wanted Diana to tell him.

His body tightened as she bent down to pick up the banjo case, displaying a grace and unconscious sensuality that sent his blood pressure soaring. What was it about her that caught his imagination and attracted him as no other woman had?

He wasn't given a chance to think about the answer. Abe was asking him a question, so he tore his gaze away from Diana to pay attention to his host.

A little while later, Strauss and Diana walked toward the couch where Michael and Abe were seated. Abe broke off their conversation abruptly when he saw them approaching, making Diana wonder what the two men had been discussing.

Michael stood and shook hands with Strauss as Diana introduced him.

"Who won?" Michael asked.

"It was a tie," replied Strauss in an upper-class English accent. Putting his arm around Diana's shoulders, he added, "This wretched child takes unfair advantage by being so beautiful, I can't concentrate."

Michael wanted to knock the other man's arm off Diana, but managed to control the urge. "You both play very well."

"I taught her everything she knows," Strauss said, grinning broadly.

Smiling, Diana purred, "Fortunately, I learned more."

"Oh, charming," Strauss said indignantly. He removed his arm and handed Diana over to Michael. "Here, mate. Take this ungrateful wench. I want nothing more to do with her." He grabbed Abe's arm and began to drag him away. Over his shoulder, he contradicted himself by saying, "See you next month, love. You'd better practice. I plan to win next time."

Diana laughed. Looking up at Michael, she said, "I hope you weren't too bored."

"Boredom is impossible around you."

He took her hand, and saw her flinch when his fingers closed around hers. He lifted her hand. There were red marks on the tips of each finger of her left hand.

"My fingers got soft because I haven't played for a while," she explained as his jaw tightened and some fierce emotion flared in his eyes.

"Why didn't you stop playing when your fingers began to hurt?"

She shrugged. "A few sore fingers aren't that big a deal."

"But winning is?"

"I like to *try* to win. My father once told me that we can't always expect to get the brass ring, but we can certainly reach out and try to grab it."

"You haven't said much about your family. I'd like to hear about the people responsible for creating you."

"They live in Palm Springs."

He waited for more, but she had apparently said all she was going to on the subject of her parents. It wasn't much.

"Would you like something, to eat?" she asked instead. "We can elbow our way through to the buffet table."

A young couple appeared in front of them, as if they had just popped out of a bottle. The girl's hair looked as though it had been combed with an egg beater, and she wore an earring in one ear that matched the one the boy wore in one of his ears. Michael guessed they were in their late teens and trying to look older, but had ended up looking much younger. They introduced themselves as Chick and Charlie; announced they were getting a group organized for charades, and invited Diana and Michael to join in.

The girl—was she Chick or Charlie? Michael wondered—added, "We've thought of some really clever song titles, all from the sixties." She giggled. "It should be a blast."

Trying to sound as though he really meant it, Michael said, "Sorry. We promised the sitter we would be home early."

He heard a sound from Diana, but ignored it. With a no-nonsense grip on her arm, he steered a course through the meandering masses toward the door. Once outside, he took a deep breath. It had stopped raining, and the night air was clear and clean. Diana was quiet, too quiet. He stopped walking and looked at her.

Her head was tilted to one side as she studied him . . . and she was smiling. No, she was grinning. "You're not mad," he said, amazed.

"Why would I be mad?"

"Because I yanked you away from the party."

"Your exit line was a little startling, but imaginative," she said with amusement. "I take it you're not wild about charades."

"Diana," he began hesitantly, "I might as well be honest. I hate parties."

"If you hate parties, why did you agree to go tonight?"

"Because you were going to be there." He began walking away from the Piccolos' houseboat, taking her along with him, his fingers laced through hers.

As they walked, his softly spoken words hung in the air between them. The only sounds in the night were their footsteps and the lapping of water against the hulls of the houseboats.

With each step bringing them closer to her home, Diana felt tension tighten deep inside her. In a few minutes she was going to have to choose whether or not to take the giant step toward an intimate relationship with Michael. She was torn between wanting to give in to the delicious torment of desire he created within her, and the feeling that she should resist the claim he would make, not only on her body, but on her independence as well.

She had her freedom now. No one told her what to do but her own conscience. If she committed herself to Michael, there was a chance she would find herself relying on another person for her happiness instead of herself. She wasn't sure she was ready to take that chance.

When they reached the door to her houseboat, she stopped and looked up at him. She felt the need to make some kind of qualifying statement. "We haven't known each other very long."

He touched the side of her face with his free hand. "I'm trying to change that. The only way I know how to do that is to spend as much time as possible together."

"Like going to a party you hate."

"If necessary, yes." A corner of his mouth curved up into a faint smile. "It wasn't that big a sacrifice. How else would I have learned you play a mean banjo and like to crawl out windows?"

Diana was unusually hesitant. "Would you like to come in for a cup of coffee?"

His thumb stroked her bottom lip. "No."

He was giving her conflicting signals, and she was at a loss. "But I thought—"

"Diana, I want to go inside, but not for a cup of coffee," he said quietly. "I want to be inside you."

She caught her breath. "And I pride myself on plain speaking."

He kissed her briefly. "My wanting to make love to you can't come as any great surprise," he murmured against her mouth.

The weight of his body pressed her back against the door, his hands supporting him on the hard surface. A swirl of molten heat wrapped around her as he forced her lips apart to feed his growing hunger.

She gasped his name when his mouth released hers to move to her soft, tempting throat. Any protest she was about to make melted away as he leaned his lower body against hers, sending white-hot spirals of desire through her.

His warm hands moved to the sides of her face. His breath brushed against her mouth as he murmured, "Unlock your door, moon goddess. Let me in."

He pressed short, almost desperate kisses on her lips as his leg moved between hers. "Let me in," he repeated huskily, giving more than one meaning to his plea.

"Michael." She sighed achingly. "I'm not sure I'm ready for this."

"Yes, you are. I can feel how ready you are."

His hands slid down between their bodies to glide over her breasts, pausing to stroke their hard tips. For a long moment he looked down at her, watching her incredible eyes reflect her emotions. Her body was trembling as his hands moved slowly over her. Then her eyes closed as she absorbed the tremor rippling through her.

Michael knew he was rushing her, but he needed to know she was his. He wanted her to need him, only him . . . for more than physical satisfaction, but that would do for a start.

After a final, deep kiss, he pushed himself off her. "It's up to you, Diana. You're a lady who likes choices. This is one for you to make."

Diana couldn't tear her gaze away from his. He was leaving the decision up to her, but she didn't feel she was capable of making a rational decision at that moment. She wanted him too badly.

Her fingers trembled as she fished her keys from the pocket of her dress. When she had difficulty performing the simple act of slipping the key into the lock, his hand closed over hers.

"I'll do it. I'll take care of everything."

Feeling incredibly weak, she let her head fall onto his shoulder, needing the support of his arm around her and the strength of his body. There wasn't room for doubt or indecision in her passion-drugged mind. This craving eating away at her was too powerful, consuming any sensible thought.

He shut the door behind them and relocked it. Her keys were tossed onto a small table by the door. Then his hands delved through her hair to hold her head still as his mouth covered hers hungrily.

In the far recesses of her mind Diana was aware that Michael was slowly moving them toward her bedroom. His tongue plunged deep in her mouth, and her hands clung to his shoulders and slid around his neck. Low moans of ecstasy vibrated deep in her throat as his mouth worked its magic spell.

When Michael heard and felt her immediate response, his control slipped dangerously, and he forced himself to slow down. He had to make it good for her, to take care of her. He didn't want her to regret giving herself to him. Her pleasure was as important to him as his own.

Diana felt cool air brush her heated flesh as her dress fell away under Michael's experienced hands. She felt no last-minute panic or fear, only a passionate pull on her senses. She was caught up in the consuming fire in her blood, stoked by his hands flowing across her throbbing breasts, over her waist, and gliding lower.

With trembling hands she pushed his sport coat off his shoulders, and it joined her dress in a crumpled heap on the floor. Her fingers became so uncoordinated, she was unable to perform the simple action of unbuttoning his shirt. Sighing softly with frustration, she raised her dazed eyes to his.

His smile was both triumphant and tender, his hands possessive as they smoothed over her silken skin. "It's all right, honey," he said soothingly. "Just hold on to me. I'll do the rest." The scrap of material clothing her lower body was swept away. Then he picked her up and lifted her onto the bed.

Her gaze never left his tall form as he quickly shed his clothes. He joined her on the bed, pulling her against his hard body, and her eyes closed as a flood of delicious sensations flowed through her.

A soft sound escaped her parted lips, igniting the banked fires deep inside him. She was so breathtakingly responsive. He knew the supreme pleasure of being wanted by this extraordinary woman. Her hips arched under his hand as he caressed her intimately, and his mouth claimed her parted lips again and again. He shuddered violently. Lord, he thought. He was going to shatter into a million pieces when he took her.

"Hang on to me, moon goddess. Don't let go. I feel like I'm going to fly away."

With a single, lithe motion he moved over her and began to enter her, forcing himself to go slowly. There was no resistance, though, and when she lifted her hips in a wordless plea, he filled her completely. His groan of extreme pleasure was echoed by hers as they came together.

Finally this elusive woman was his. He had needed a claim on her, and right now he had to be satisfied with this physical claim. Right now it was enough. Her body clenched him deep inside her, and his blood boiled. Oh, God, it was more than enough. It was everything.

They climbed the summit of need together and fell over the edge into a chasm of exquisite satisfaction.

After a long interval, Michael found the strength to pull the quilt at the foot of the bed up to cover their cooling bodies. She murmured something—his name? —and sighed with contentment as she snuggled her head against his sholder. He tucked her soft body against him, feeling the need to keep her close to him. Along with ease in his body was the ease in his mind regarding Miss Diana Dragas. One barrier had been breached. It was a start.

Six

Usually Diana woke quickly, ready to face the day as soon as she opened her eyes. This Sunday morning was an exception. She felt deliciously lazy, and reluctant to leave the cozy cocoon of her bed. Nuzzling her face into her pillow, she tried to ignore the tempting aroma of freshly brewed coffee.

Her eyes blinked open. The scent of coffee?

Michael.

She rolled onto her back, turning her head. The other side of her bed was empty. The covers had been tossed back and the pillow was softly indented where his head had lain. Memories of the passion-filled night washed over her in vivid detail. She closed her eyes as she remembered the pleasure he had given her. On the heels of pleasure, though, came reality.

Well, you've done it this time, she chided herself. You've gone to bed with a man you've only known for several days . . . and to top it off, you've fallen in love with him. Or was it that she had made love with him because she loved him? Whatever. There wasn't a single doubt in her mind about her feelings. She was in love with Michael Dare. She didn't want to be, but she was. Now what are you going to do? she asked herself.

Since the answer wasn't forthcoming, she flipped the covers back and grabbed her robe. Tying the sash around her waist, she ventured out from behind the partition.

Michael was dressed in his slacks and white shirt which he hadn't bothered to button. He was pouring himself a cup of coffee. Apparently sensing her presence, he looked over his shoulder and saw her standing near the partition. He took another earthenware mug from the cupboard and filled it with steaming coffee.

He brought it over to her, leaning down to kiss her briefly.

"Good morning," he said.

"Hmmm."

"Are you usually this talkative in the morning?"

She walked over to the couch and sat down at one end, folding her legs under her. "I'm not one to go around talking to myself. I'm usually alone when I wake up."

"Good," he said with satisfaction as he returned to the kitchen counter.

"I see you managed to figure out how the coffee maker works," she said. For some strange reason that irked her.

He turned to look at her, detecting the bite in her voice. "I watched you make coffee the other day." His eyes narrowed. "What's wrong? Is this your usual grumpy nature in the morning or is it something else?"

She scowled at him. "Do you usually make yourself at home in someone else's place after spending the night?"

"No," he answered bluntly, wondering why she was asking. "I just leave."

"Why am I the exception?"

Michael wasn't ready to answer that question and knew that, in her present mood, she wasn't ready to hear his answer anyway. He asked a question of his own. "Are you angry because I'm puttering around in your kitchen without asking your permission?"

"I don't know," she replied honestly. "I'm no expert on the proper behavior of mornings after the night before." Her tone implied he was. "I told you I don't go in for casual affairs. This is new to me."

"You'll get used to it." He turned away so she couldn't see his tight expression. If she thought she was having a casual affair now, he had some news for her. Last night had been anything but casual, but now was not the time to convince her otherwise. He would reassure her as they went along. They needed time together, and he was going to see they got it.

Diana watched as Michael opened the refrigerator door and took out several jars and some packets of lunch meat as though it were his kitchen.

"Now what are you doing?" she asked.

"Making a picnic lunch."

"Oh, really? Who's going on a picnic?"

His glance in her direction was amused. "We are. Do you like mustard or mayonnaise with ham?"

"Both." She stood up and walked into the kitchen. On the table in the breakfast nook was her wicker picnic basket. Inside, along with the plastic dishes that fit into the cover, were a bag of potato chips, a jar of pickles, two apples, and a bag of marshmallows. He'd had a busy morning.

Placing her empty mug in the sink, she said, "I don't remember being asked to go on a picnic."

He slapped several pieces of ham on a slice of bread, set another slice on top, deftly sliced the sandwich in half, and added it to the stack of sandwiches he had already made. "You were asleep when I thought of it."

"I'm awake now."

He smiled at her, purposely not asking her to go on the picnic. She might refuse him out of principle. "So you are." He wiped his hands on a towel, then looped it around her neck and tugged on the ends to bring her closer.

His breath was warm against her mouth, and she was melting against him before he even kissed her. This time his kiss was deeper and more intimate. She leaned into him, reveling in the exotic taste of him. Dammit! she thought. He was making her forget the point she was trying to make. He untied the sash and parted her robe, and she sighed into his mouth as his hands found her bare breasts.

Her arms raised to encircle his neck. Later she would complain about his dictatorial attitude. These particular activities were not designed for philosophical discussions. It didn't seem appropriate to strike out for equality, either, while climbing the pinnacle of passion, or afterward, when they were taking a lengthy shower together.

It wasn't until they were seated at a picnic table under a tree at Stinson Beach that Diana remembered Michael was guilty of directing their day without any input from her.

"Michael, I'm curious about something."

"Pass me the pickles. What are you curious about?"

She handed him the jar of pickles. "Do you usually expect everyone to fall in with your plans automatically, or am I the only one who gets that treatment?"

He calmly munched on a dill pickle. "Could you be more specific?"

"You took it for granted I wanted to go on a picnic today. I might have had plans of my own."

"Are you enjoying the picnic?"

"Yes, but—"

"Did you have other plans for today?"

"No, but—"

"Did you want to spend the day with me?"

"Yes, but—"

"So what's the problem?"

She scowled at him. "I don't like being told what to do," she said heatedly. "I'm the lady who likes choices, remember? I don't like being taken for granted." She tilted her head slightly as she studied him. "Directing documentaries must be second nature to you, since you like to control everything around you. You probably get your bossiness from being an only child. You're used to getting your own way."

He smiled. "You're an only child too."

She gave an exasperated sigh. "Could we change the subject? I don't seem to be doing real well with this one."

He put down his sandwich and reached over to take her hand. "I think we'd better discuss this now. You're right. I've been as subtle as a tank where you're concerned. My only excuse is I've been on my own for a long time and I'm not used to considering anyone else but myself. I'll try to be more considerate in the future." His voice was sincere, his expression serious.

"I can't ask for more than that," she said. "Maybe I shouldn't be making such a big issue out of this, but I was always directed so firmly while I was growing up. I don't want to go back to having my life completely governed by someone else."

Michael suddenly realized what the fuss had been about that morning. She was afraid! It gave him the confidence he hadn't known before with her. She had as many insecurities about their relationship as he had, maybe more. "There are bound to be adjustments in any relationship. Also compromises. We have all the time in the world to work out any and all difficulties that come up."

Diana let out a painful breath, unaware that she had been holding it while he spoke. "Do we have a relationship?"

His fingers tightened around her hand. "I certainly am involved in one with you. Last night I got the impression you were more than a little involved with me too. Or was I wrong?"

She shook her head slowly. "You weren't wrong," she said softly. The wind off the ocean tousled his hair slightly, and she imagined running her own hands through his hair, kissing him, touching him. . . .

His thumb brushed across the back of her hand. "Diana, if you keep looking at me like that, we're liable to embarrass those elderly people sitting at the table next to ours." He smiled tenderly as heightened color tinted her cheeks. "If it's any consolation, I would like to touch more than just your hand too. Here." He withdrew his hand and grabbed the bag of marshmallows. "Have one of these for dessert."

She suddenly laughed, the moment of tension dissolved by his unexpected remark. She extracted a soft, powdery marshmallow from the bag and examined the squishy object closely. "I've had to eat some unusual dishes at official functions, but I can honestly say I've never been served a marshmallow for dessert."

"You're a food taster as well as a translator?" he asked.

Finishing the marshmallow, she licked her fingers to stall before she answered his question. She could let him think she had been at official dinners as a translator, but that wouldn't be the truth. He was a man who strove for honesty in his work. He deserved nothing less from her.

"My father was in the diplomatic corps. Occasionally my mother and I were expected to attend certain functions with him. One instruction I was given was to eat whatever I was served, no matter how strange it looked or tasted. The dishes served were usually specialties of the country we were in."

"Would it cause an international incident if you

refused to eat jellied eels or something just as repulsive?"

She smiled. "Don't let my mother hear you call jellied eels repulsive. She loves them."

Leaning both arms on the table, he pressed her for more. "Tell me about your familly."

"Why?"

He saw her stiffen, and knew he had poked a sensitive nerve. "Your parents sound like interesting people. I told you about my family. I'd like to hear about yours."

She gave her stock answer. "I don't talk about my family, especially to journalists."

It was the wrong thing to say. "I'm your lover, dammit, not some anonymous reporter."

He became aware of the sudden interest in their conversation by the elderly couple sitting at the other picnic table. He flung his long legs over the bench of their table and strode around to the other side. With a grip of steel, he propelled Diana to her feet and strode angrily toward the beach, forcing her to come along with him.

They passed several family groups sitting on the sand and a couple of teenagers sprawled on towels with a radio blaring. Michael kept walking until they were far enough away from other people to have a private conversation.

He placed both of his hands on her shoulders and stared down at her. "Diana, I don't *have* to know about your family. I have a feeling whatever it is you don't want to tell me is tied up with your hostility toward journalists, and I would like to think you can trust me enough by now to tell me about it. I'm a man first, your lover second, and a journalist third. Talk to me as the first two and forget the third."

The breeze off the ocean was moist and smelled of the sea. It blew Diana's hair away from her face as she looked out at the limitless horizon. Her voice was low and strained. "It's not easy for me to talk about my family."

"It's not easy for me to feel shut out, either." He dropped his hands. It was obvious she was going through some kind of inner struggle, and all he could do was wait. She would either confide in him or she wouldn't.

Still looking out at the sea, she said, "It's become a habit for me not to say anything about my family. Words can't be printed or twisted if I don't say them. Now you want those words."

He watched some shore birds scurry over the damp sand as waves receded. He waited. His silence spoke more loudly than words.

"My father is Nicholas Dragas."

He turned his head, his expression blank. He made no comment. He had already figured that out for himself, from putting several of her comments together and jogging his memory, but he had wanted to hear it from her.

She took a deep breath before continuing. "Eight years ago my father befriended a young Russian diplomat who was in love with an American girl. The Russian wanted to take her home, and asked my father to help with the paper work and some of the political cogs and wheels."

A thread of anger entered her voice. "Some enterprising reporter decided to create news where none existed. He wrote a charming article claiming an American diplomat and a Russian diplomat were involved in a homosexual affair."

A sharp curse escaped from Michael.

"Exactly. To make a long, unpleasant story short, my father was politely asked to resign from the diplomatic corps, the Russian was sent back to the Soviet Union without his lady love . . ."

"And the news media sharpened their pencils on the whole family," Michael finished for her.

"Bingo. In bold type, small print, and with as many pictures as they could get. There was even an old photo of me on one of my grandfather's horses in Sussex. Don't ask me where they dug it up from. I believe I was six or seven. My father was standing alongside the horse, with his hand on the back of my waist. Do you want to know what the caption said?"

"I have a feeling you're going to tell me."

" 'Dragas likes little girls, too.' "

Another expletive cut into the salt air. Michael threaded his fingers through hers and started walking along the beach. Now he knew why she hated newsmen . . . and he couldn't really blame her, under the circumstances. When he had realized who her father was, he had vaguely remembered notoriety of some kind connected with Nicholas Dragas, but hadn't been able to recall the nature of the scandal.

Now that she had started talking about her family, Diana found it surprisingly easy to go on. "My mother is from an upper-class home in England, where appearances count for a great deal. All of the publicity was very hard on her. I used to get so angry when I saw the tears in her eyes, her chin up as she went through the barrage of reporters every time she and my father left the house. She was being torn to bits inside, but wouldn't give the public the satisfaction of seeing it on her face."

"What do your parents do now?"

"My father dabbles in real estate and my mother plays golf and bridge. They seem reasonably content with their quiet life. I think my father still wants to clear his name. The last time I was home he mentioned he was thinking about writing a book to explain the truth, but my mother strongly opposed the idea. She didn't want everything stirred up again."

"How do you feel about it?"

Diana gazed out at the undulating waves of the ocean, where the sunlight glistened like tiny diamonds on the surface. "I can sympathize with both of them. My father's reputation was given a public battering, few people believing in his innocence. Only friends like Rena and Abe unconditionally stuck by him. I can also see my mother's side of it. After all she's been through in the past, she certainly doesn't want the whole mess to start up again." She looked up at Michael, a faint smile shaping her mouth. "So now you know about my family. Not a very pretty story to tell, but there it is."

He stopped and turned to face her, lifting her hand up to his mouth. "Thank you for telling me, Diana. It means a great deal to me to have your trust, for you to let me get close to you. There shouldn't be any secrets between us."

Her expression was serious as she looked up at him. "I've never told anyone else. I'm not sure why I told you."

His smile was tender, his touch gentle as he pulled her into his arms. "You're a smart lady. You'll figure it out."

Disregarding the other people on the beach, he kissed her. His mouth slanted over hers to take a brief sample of her essence. At least he had intended for the kiss to be brief. When she responded and her tongue met his, the spiral of desire began to tighten in his body.

Before things got out of hand, he raised his head and took her hand again. "We'd better keep walking," he said in a strangled voice. "We might end up giving these nature lovers more than they bargained for." As though talking more to himself than to her, he added, "You're more than I bargained for, too, moon goddess."

Turning back the way they had come, he gestured

out toward the water with his free hand. "Have you ever heard about the Stinson sea serpent?"

She accepted the change of subject for what it was, a postponement. They were spark to tinder each time their lips met. Now wasn't the time or the place to let the blaze flare out of control.

"Is there such a thing?" she asked.

"Some people think so. In 1983 a crew of road workers saw a snakelike creature resembling the Loch Ness Monster out in the water. A number of other people swear they've seen it too. The so-called experts put it down to wave action, sun glare, or dolphins."

"It sounds like you've done a lot of research on the Stinson sea serpent. Is that going to be the subject of your next documentary?"

How odd, Michael thought. Now she was discussing his work naturally, without any digs or bitterness, and he was the one who didn't want to talk about it. Especially after Abe Piccolo's suggestion of the night before to meet to discuss the "Where Are They Now?" documentary. Somehow Abe had found out about it, and was interested in appearing in it. Diana was loyal to her friends, and protective of them. Michael wasn't sure she would approve of Abe's involvement in the documentary. Their relationship was still too new and fragile to test with something she strongly opposed. Publicity was what Abe Piccolo wanted, but Diana might not see it that way. Perhaps she would feel Abe was being exploited and Michael was the exploiter.

He had to give her some kind of answer. "Myths and monsters aren't in my line. It's just one of those bits of trivia I've picked up." He gazed down at her, his eyes amused. "I thought the Stinson sea serpent was more interesting than the weather."

"It sure is." A Frisbee went sailing by, and as she dodged, she bumped into him. She laughed. "Sorry."

His dark eyes collided with her brilliant turquoise

ones as she grabbed hold of his arm to keep her balance. The impact of her soft body sent a wild hunger rippling through him.

This woman was going to make him old before his time.

Diana's breath caught when she saw the dark secrets and tantalizing promise in his eyes. She had never considered herself to be a sensual person, but Michael had only to look at her and she was alive with desires she never knew could exist in one body.

He gave her an ironic smile and tugged at her hand to continue walking.

They strolled along the shore until they came to a volleyball game in progress. One of the players called out to them to join the game, and Michael gave Diana a questioning look. With a wide smile and a nod, she quickly slipped off her shoes.

A couple of hours later Diana sank down on the sand a safe distance from the action. After a few minutes Michael collapsed beside her.

Lying back in the sand, he groaned. "Lord, I'm getting old."

Her arms wrapped around her knees, Diana continued to watch the game. "They take their volleyball seriously, don't they?"

"That giant in the orange shorts had my name on every ball he hit. He must not like old people."

Chuckling, she glanced at him over her shoulder. His eyes were shut. "You poor old thing. You're all of, what, thirty-five, thirty-six?"

He opened one eye and said sourly, "Thirty-four."

"I guess you wouldn't want to go hiking on Mt. Tamalpais, then, would you?"

Both eyes opened wide, and he gave her a look of horror. "You've got to be kidding."

"As a matter of fact, I am." She leaned down on one elbow beside him. "May I ask you something?"

"As long as you don't ask me to move."

"I was wondering what you usually do on Sundays." She smiled impishly. "It doesn't look like you spend the day doing strenuous exercise."

"I work."

His bald statement held no emotion. It was a fact, neither embroidered on nor explained.

Diana wanted an explanation. "On Sundays? Why?"

"I don't have anything better to do."

"Hogwash."

He made a choking sound that could have been a strangled laugh or an exclamation of surprise. He propped himself up on his arms. "What do you mean, hogwash?"

"You work because you love it. The competition, the challenge, the work itself. I saw your face when you were playing volleyball. The harder the guy in the orange shorts hit the ball at you, the harder you worked to return it. I heard the pride in your voice when you were defending your occupation the other day. Your work is very important to you."

He considered what she said for a moment. Then he asked, "Since you seem to have me pegged, why wasn't I working yesterday or today? Why did I spend that time with you?"

She dug her hand into the sand and let the tiny grains trickle through her fingers. "I haven't figured that out yet. Do you deny I'm right? You are an ambitious man. Why not admit it?"

"All right, I admit it. Do you feel better?"

In a clipped English accent, she said politely, "Yes, thank you. Quite."

His low chuckle turned into deep laughter of pure pleasure. He fell back on the sand, holding his side.

"What's so blasted funny?" she asked indignantly, sitting up and glaring down at him.

"Sorry," he said, grinning broadly. "It just struck me funny when you turned into a proper English madam."

He sat up too. "You are so many women all wrapped up in one delightful package. I never know which one I'll see next."

One of his hands stole around her neck, and she knew he wanted to kiss her. "Michael! There're other people all around us."

He was about to say something when the giant in the orange shorts trotted over to them. Michael noted sourly that the man wasn't even breathing heavily after playing another rousing game.

"Hey, come on, sport," the giant said. "We're starting up another game." He grinned. "We'll take it easy on you this time."

Michael stood and looked up, way up, at the man. "You'll have to play without me, sport. It's time for my heart pills."

Orange shorts turned to Diana. "How about you, sweetie?"

She shook her head, trying hard not to laugh. "I have to go with him. I'm his nurse at the old folks' home."

The giant shrugged and left, and, grinning, Michael extended his hand down to her. They retrieved their shoes and left the energetic volleyball game behind them. It didn't take them long to gather up the remnants of their picnic, and then they were on their way.

Since they weren't dressed to go out to eat, they stopped to get a bucket of chicken for dinner. Back at her houseboat, Diana spread a red-and-white-checkered tablecloth on the floor of the living room area, moving the coffee table out of the way first. She set out several thick candles and paper plates, then put a record on. Michael expected music of some kind, but heard instead wind rustling through pine trees, birds twittering away, a bubbling brook, and a few other nature sounds he couldn't positively identify.

Diana settled down on the tablecloth and gestured for him to join her.

"Another picnic?" he asked as he sat cross-legged.

Reaching for a piece of chicken, she said, "One of the lessons I was taught about entertaining was that atmosphere is very important in order to have a successful, interesting meal. Food is supposed to taste better when presented properly. Of course, the right combination of guests is important as well."

"From what you've told me about your mother, I can't see her sitting on the floor eating chicken with her fingers."

Diana handed him a bottle of wine she had dug out of a cupboard. "I don't follow her rules to the letter," she admitted with a grin. "The corkscrew is on your left."

As he was opening the wine, he said mildly, "I think you go out of your way to bend the rules, a sort of rebellion from your years of having to conform. No conventional apartment for you, no nine-to-five job. I bet your car isn't a sedate compact, either."

"I don't own a car."

"It figures," he said dryly. "Why don't you own a car?"

She accepted a glass of wine from him. "I couldn't afford one when I first arrived here, and later, when I could, I realized I had gotten along just fine without one. I take the ferry to San Francisco, then use the cable cars, taxis, or walk."

"You can use mine while I'm gone."

She wasn't sure which startled her more, the casual offer of the use of his prize possession or the fact that he was going away. "Where . . . when are you leaving?"

"I'm taking a flight in the morning to Los Angeles. There's an awards banquet Monday evening, and I'm going to pick up an award for my documentary on homeless people."

Her eyes lit up with pleasure. "That's wonderful, Michael."

He shrugged off her praise. "So do you want to use my car while I'm gone?"

"No. Thank you for offering, but I don't need it." She smiled. "You don't want to be worrying about the condition of your car while you're in Los Angeles."

"Come with me."

His quiet invitation was tempting, very tempting, but she couldn't accept. The regret was evident in her voice. "I can't. I have commitments I can't get out of."

He had expected her to refuse, but the disappointment was there just the same. "I'm not sure I have to say this, but I want to make it clear I won't be seeing any other woman while I'm away from you. I don't expect you to go out with any other man."

She felt as though she had arrived unexpectedly at a crossroads and was unsure which fork in the road to take. "Michael," she said hesitantly, "we haven't known each other a week. It's a little soon to be staking a claim, isn't it?"

"I believe I did that last night," he said evenly. "Just in case you forgot." Reaching over, he took her wine out of her hand and set it aside, then lowered her onto the tablecloth-covered floor.

There wasn't any time to protest, even if she had wanted to. His lips pried hers apart instantly, impatiently, and she yielded to the passion that had been simmering in both of them all day. His arms slid under her, and he rolled over to cushion her soft body from the hard floor with his own.

His hands delved into her hair as his mouth moved on hers, his tongue dancing a sensual rhythm with hers. His breathing was ragged, his hands restless and searching over the fine lines of her back, hips, and thighs. He broke away from her compelling mouth to seek the sweet flavor of her throat.

"How am I going to leave you, Diana?" he asked

huskily. "You're like a fire in my blood. I want you now. I'll want you when I'm deep inside you and I'll want you after I've had you."

She gasped at the deep hunger she heard in his voice, her senses responding to the need she could feel in his hands and the heavy, throbbing masculinity under her. Nothing had ever been as exhilarating as knowing Michael wanted her.

Her hands shook slightly as she stroked his firm jaw. "Last week at this time, I didn't even know you. Now . . ."

"Now," he breathed against her lips, "you know me very well." His hands pressed her hips into his. "And you'll know me even better after tonight."

Seven

When her phone rang late Monday night, Diana didn't get out of her warm bubble bath. Her answering machine could take the call. It was probably a wrong number, anyway. Michael would be at the awards banquet and her parents wouldn't be calling at this hour. The rest of the world could leave a message. There was nothing short of a three-alarm fire that would entice her away from her bath. It had been a hectic, frenzied day, and the thought of her porcelain, claw-footed tub filled with her favorite jasmine-scented oil and gobs of frothy bubbles had kept her going.

That wretched Melanie at the agency had scheduled three separate jobs as interpreter so close together, Diana had been worn to a frazzle getting to each one on time. Naturally, they had been scattered all over the city. At the end of the day she had stopped off at the agency to give Melanie a few pointers on scheduling future assignments, then had gone out to eat with her and several others who worked for the agency. What with everyone sharing various complaints and exchanging experiences—and two strawberry daiquiris—Diana hadn't gotten home until a little after eleven.

By the time the bubbles had faded, so had her irritation. She slipped into her kimono and left the steamy bathroom to get a glass of milk. Passing the answering machine, she saw the blinking red light and rewound the tape.

Michael's voice shattered the silence. "Hi, moon goddess. My Rolex watch says it's eleven-thirty. Where the hell are you? Have a good excuse ready when I see you on Wednesday."

She played the message back again just to hear his voice. Finally she switched off the machine. She wandered over to the window overlooking the bay. Darn that man! She missed him. Miss Independent missed Michael Dare, the journalist. If this nagging emptiness because he wasn't with her was love, it wasn't the moonlight and roses it was cracked up to be.

Staring out at the black velvet night, she felt another strange emotion. Was it loneliness? She didn't remember every feeling this particular way before, but she recognized it nonetheless.

With one last look at the dark water, she muttered some satisfying curses in several languages and headed for her bed.

Her schedule was lighter on Tuesday. After she taught the English class for high-school students, she took the ferry home.

The only message on her answering machine was from the agency, with an assignment for the following week, another court appearance. This time she would be interpreting for a German man who spoke a little English, but not enough to get him through involved legal questions. She had translated for Mr. Burkhardt several times before, when he had met with his lawyer to discuss the suit he was bringing against a local car dealership. He was a bull-chested, short man with an equally short temper, but Diana liked him. It was a case of David going against Goliath, and Mr. Burkhardt was prepared with a few slingshots of proof to inflict at least a few wounds on the dealership's reputation for fair deals and service, if not to knock down his powerful opponent.

After she had marked down the time and location, Diana went into the bedroom to change her clothes. As she passed her dresser, she turned on the cassette tape player sitting on top of it. A man's voice spoke a sentence in English, repeated it in Japanese, then paused to give Diana time to try it.

Her attempt at the Japanese phrase was muffled as she pulled a top over her head. She was fastening her jeans when she heard her front door close and her father call out her name.

She stabbed the off button on the cassette player and hurried out of her bedroom. "Dad! What are you doing here?"

She was wrapped in a bear hug; and then her father held her away so he could look down at her. "Why do you leave your door open? Why don't you just put a 'Come on in, mugger' sign on your front door?"

"No fair answering a question with a question."

"I'm here to see my favorite girl—next to your mother, that is. She sends you her love, by the way."

Smiling warmly at her father, Diana was pleased to see he looked well. He wore gray slacks and a charcoal sport coat over a cream-colored shirt. His once-black hair was now more white than gray, a concession to his age of seventy years. He had become a father at forty-six, later than most of his contemporaries.

She tugged on his arm, leading him over to the couch, and he sat down beside her. "I hope you don't mind," he said, "but I've invited Rena and Abe to dine with us. Rena was making threatening noises about a new recipe for beef stroganoff, and I neglected to pack any Alka-Seltzer. We could go out if your larder can't be stretched that far."

"I have plenty on hand," she said easily. "It's wonderful to see you, Dad, but why didn't you let me know you were coming?"

"I decided on the spur of the moment. I got a call from Abe about . . . a business deal, and decided to come look into it."

She raised an eyebrow. "Abe is becoming interested in real estate?"

Looking anywhere but at his daughter, Nicholas answered evasively, "It's too early to say. I have a bone to pick with you, young lady," he continued, changing the subject. "What is this I hear about a serious involvement with Michael Dare? And why do I hear about it from Rena, and not from you? You didn't even mention his name in your last letter."

Diana's mouth twisted into a grimace. "I didn't even *know* him when I wrote my last letter."

"A whirlwind romance?" Nicholas asked gently.

She hugged one of the throw pillows to her chest. "The whirlwind part describes it nicely."

"Rena and Abe seem to think it's serious between you two. Is it?"

Diana felt hunted. Her father was asking questions she wasn't ready to answer. "It's too early to say. I only met him last week."

"It took me two days after meeting your mother to realize I wanted to see her lovely face across the breakfast table for the rest of my life."

She was oddly moved by her father's admission. "Did she feel the same?"

"Believe it or not, it took her a whole week to come to her senses. You know how careful your mother is. It takes her a week to pack for a weekend trip."

"I must take after you, then," Diana said quietly, giving away more than she had intended.

"Don't bite your lip, darling. It's such an unattractive habit."

She laughed. "You sound like Mother."

"Your mother is a wise woman. I'm sure she would handle this better than I am."

"Handle what?"

"Well, obviously there are difficulties in this new relationship or you wouldn't be hugging that pillow and biting your lip. I haven't seen you this strung out since the time you bought the strapless gown to wear on your first date with that Austrian boy."

Diana tossed the pillow onto the couch to prove she didn't need it. "My chief concern was whether or not the blasted dress would stay where it was supposed to. At sixteen, I didn't have a great deal to support it."

Nicholas cleared his throat. "Yes. Well . . . If I remember correctly, your mother made you march back upstairs to change. That's what I mean when I said she knows how to handle this sort of thing. So what are the problems? And don't tell me there aren't any." Going right for the jugular, he asked bluntly, "Is it because of his occupation?"

She sighed. "It was at first. I guess it still is, in a way, although he isn't a reporter like . . ." Her voice trailed off.

"Like the vultures who circled around us eight years ago? You can say it, darling. I don't mind talking about the past."

"*I* don't like to talk about it," she said quietly.

Her father shifted sideways in order to see her face more clearly. Taking one of her hands in his, he asked, "Do you remember going to that dentist in Germany? The one who slapped you when you accidentally bit his finger while he was examining you?"

"Dad, for Pete's sake, Michael isn't a dentist."

"Bear with me. I'm trying to make a point. A trifle clumsily, perhaps, but answer my question."

"Yes." She sighed, going along with whatever he was leading to. "I remember the dentist."

"Your one bad experience with a dentist didn't put you off all dentists. In fact, I believe you were quite fond of the one in England."

"It's hardly the same thing," she said crossly.

"Yes, I believe it is." He released her hand. "Think about it. You've met many people while we traveled around the world. Some imperfect, some extraordinary, some famous, some rather unpleasant chaps, and a few women who couldn't be classed as ladies. We always told you to judge each individual, no matter what his culture, on his own merits. I believe this Michael Dare deserves that same privilege." Patting her knee, he added, "Enough of the lectures. Abe and Rena will be over soon. I'll help you peel the spuds."

"Spuds?" Shaking her head, she laughed. "You've never peeled a spud in your life. Do you even know what a spud is?"

He stood up and grinned. "I do believe it is a potato," he said in imitation of his wife's crisp, English tones. In his own voice he added, "Come along, child. Lead me to the spuds."

Her father was spared the necessity of carving up potatoes or his fingers. Diana fixed glazed chicken and rice with a leafy salad and biscuits. Knowing her father was at a complete loss in the kitchen, she wasn't at all surprised when he simply pulled out a chair from the table and began to fill her in on the things he and her mother had been doing lately.

When Rena and Abe arrived, it was like old times. The conversation was lively and colorful—past experiences, old friends, catching up on each other's lives over a good meal and a bottle of wine. By the time Diana served coffee, her father had set up the card table minus the jigsaw puzzle near the large window. Abe and her father were gin rummy fanatics, and took advantage of each visit to play.

Abe was shuffling the cards when the bell outside her front door clanged several times.

Diana walked over to the door, smiling when her father said, "Invite in whoever it is. I feel hot tonight."

As soon as she opened the door, she was grabbed and soundly kissed.

When she was allowed to breathe, she gasped, "Michael! What are you doing here?"

"You're always asking me that, and the answer is always the same." His mouth suddenly became a hard line when he heard the sound of a man's laughter from inside Diana's houseboat. "Am I interrupting anything?"

It was the first time Diana had heard him speak in that particular tone. She didn't care to hear it again. "A few minutes later and you would have."

"It's just as well I came back early, then." His voice was deadly quiet.

Moving her aside, he stormed into her house. When he caught sight of the three people in the living area, he stopped, his fury dissipating like air out of a balloon.

Rena and Abe greeted him as though he had been expected, and the other man invited him to sit down at the card table with him and Abe. Michael glanced back at Diana.

"Michael," she said, "this is my father, Nicholas Dragas. Dad, this is Michael Dare."

The two men shook hands. There was a brief summing up by both, made final when Diana's father nodded his head as if he had reached a conclusion.

"Do you play gin rummy, Mr. Dare?"

It sounded more like a challenge than an invitation. "It's been awhile."

Abe and Nicholas exchanged glances that caused Diana to laugh. The two older men were mentally rubbing their hands together, relishing a new opponent like a pair of grizzly bears licking their chops over a fat salmon.

She felt it only fair to warn Michael. "These two play a mean game of gin rummy. They've been known to draw blood, on occasion, with their sharp tactics."

Her father gave her a quelling glance. "He looks as though he can take care of himself, Diana Victoria. Don't you have something else you could be doing other than giving needless advice?"

Diana grimaced, and Michael glanced at her. "Victoria?" he asked with amusement.

"He always drags out my middle name when he wants to squash me for being cheeky."

He smiled. "It doesn't seem to work."

"You noticed that too," Nicholas said dryly. "Sit down, Mr. Dare. Ignore my child. We have a game to play."

Michael pulled out a chair and slung his jacket over its back. As he sat down across from Diana's father, he rolled up the sleeves of his light-tan shirt. "If I'm going to get trounced in this game," he said, "I prefer it to be on a first-name basis. My middle name is Christopher, in case you feel the need to use it at any time."

Nicholas laughed. "All right, Michael Christopher. You can deal first."

Rena and Diana exchanged amused glances as the men started to play. Rena dug out a needlepoint canvas from the voluminous bag she had brought with her, and settled down on the couch. Diana gathered some of the essay papers from her English class to correct and joined Rena on the other end of the couch.

Occasionally Michael would look up from the game and glance over at Diana, and they would exchange private messages only the two of them understood. Or so they thought. Diana's father wasn't so intent on the card game that he missed the silent communication between his daughter and Michael Dare.

After an hour had passed, Nicholas hinted to Diana that playing cards was thirsty work. While Rena and Diana were busy in the kitchen making coffee and rattling cups and saucers, they couldn't hear the arrangements Abe was making for the following day. It was just as well. Abe wanted to meet Michael to discuss his upcoming documentary . . . and Diana's father wished to be included in the meeting.

Michael was in a difficult position. To have Nicholas Dragas and Abe Piccolo appear on his program was tempting, but the complications their appearances might create in his relationship with Diana was also a factor. The two older men were very persuasive, however, and he found himself agreeing to meet with them.

By the time Diana came over to serve the coffee, the

subject had been changed. Nicholas was compliment-ing Michael on his documentary on homeless people.

"I read somewhere that you lived on the streets for a week as research before you filmed the documentary. Is that true?"

"Yes."

Nicholas had obviously expected Michael to elaborate a bit more. "That must have been quite an experience."

Michael lifted his cup of coffee. "Yes," he said again, and added, "It was," before taking a sip of coffee.

Abe chuckled at Nicholas's frown. "I've tried to get this young man to talk about his work, too, Nick. It's like trying to tug an anvil out of quicksand."

Clarifying his answer somewhat, Michael said, "I let my work speak for itself."

Nicholas nodded. "It's the end results that count, not the getting there."

Michael shrugged. "I suppose so. The end result is what people want to see. Whether I go without a bath or a shave for a week and eat things most people throw away is immaterial. The finished product is what's important."

There were no further comments or questions, and the men's attention returned to the game.

By eleven o'clock, the cards had been shuffled for the last time. Nicholas was declared the overall winner. Pleased with himself, the night's entertainment, and his daughter's young man, he glanced pointedly at his watch and announced it was time for old people to be in bed. Rena and Abe laughed and obediently said good night, giving Diana a kiss and a hug before departing.

Nicholas shook Michael's hand and suggested Diana walk Michael to his car.

As they strolled up the pier Michael said to her, "I feel like a teenager who's out past curfew and my date's daddy has sent me on my way."

"You have to admit he gets things done. He was called a mover and a shaker when he worked for the government. You saw traces of that tonight."

Arriving at his car, Michael didn't immediately open the door. Instead he leaned against the car and put his arms around her, bringing her unresisting body close to his.

"Did you actually live on the streets for a week?" she asked.

He frowned. "Do you really want to talk about that right now?"

"Yes."

"I'd rather you told me where you were when I phoned last night."

"Checking up on me, Michael Christopher?"

"Yes."

"I was out with some of the women from the agency."

He didn't say anything for a moment. Then he murmured, "This isn't exactly the way I had planned for this evening to end."

It was so good to be back in his arms, to feel his strength, his masculinity. "You weren't supposed to be here until tomorrow."

"I couldn't stay away." His arms tightened. He murmured almost desperately, "Oh, Diana! Kiss me!"

The sensual current pulled and tugged at them as soon as their lips met. It seemed like weeks instead of days since they had last touched.

His mouth pressed hungrily against hers, and his arms crushed her to him. His head was swimming with the scent of her, the intoxicating taste of her, the need for her.

His hands came up to cup her face as he reluctantly raised his head, his fingers threading through her hair. "How long is your father staying?"

She gripped his wrists. "I don't know," she said breathlessly. "A day or two."

"What's your schedule tomorrow?"

"Fairly light." With a smile in her eyes she hinted, "I'm free for lunch."

His body suddenly tensed. "I can't make it for lunch."

he said flatly. "How about dinner tomorrow night? We can take your father with us if he's still here."

"All right," she said softly.

She moved back a step when he dropped his hands and reached into his pocket for his keys. Puzzled by his abrupt withdrawal, she stood to one side while he opened his door and slid behind the wheel. His eyes met hers with a long, searching look she couldn't fathom; then he drove away and she slowly walked back to the houseboat. She would trade her ability to speak foreign languages for the ability to read Michael's mind. Was he having second thoughts about their relationship? Maybe he was just tired from his trip to Los Angeles.

She sighed heavily. There was such a long way to go down the road to reach the point where she understood Michael. The facts had to be faced. There might be potholes and detours along that road, and the possibility existed of never reaching her destination.

With that less-than-pleasant thought, she entered the houseboat, plastering a smile on her face for her father's benefit.

Eight

Diana got turned down for lunch again the next day.

In the morning, before she left for an appointment in San Francisco, she asked her father if he wanted to meet her somewhere for lunch. Concentrating on his breakfast, he said he and Abe were going into the city and he wasn't sure how long their business would take.

When she inquired about the type of business they were going to be involved in, her father just smiled and told her to finish her breakfast before it got cold. Since it was cold cereal, Diana thought that was a rather odd comment to make.

Her next question about how long he was going to be staying met the same fate. He gave an oblique reply, full of double-talk and evasions, tactics he had learned from years of being a diplomat, and she stared at him in confusion. What in the world was he up to? Then she shrugged mentally. If her father and Abe were getting into something they didn't want anyone to know about, it was fine with her. They were big boys and could take care of themselves. She had enough to think about as it was, so she didn't dig any further.

When she mentioned Michael's dinner invitation for that evening, she received a more positive response. His acceptance of the invitation was an indication he would be staying at least one more night.

Or so she thought.

She had been home for half an hour when her father returned at six with the news that he had booked a flight for nine o'clock that evening. She was disappointed he would be leaving so soon, but she was also flexible. Years of working around her father's schedule had made her able to adapt at a moment's notice: emergencies, changes of time for serving dinner, holidays, and any other occasion or situation that sprang up in a family's daily life.

"I'm not sure when Michael is arriving," she said, "but I can fix something here and then we can take you out to the airport."

"No need. We can still dine out and go directly to the airport after dinner."

"But, Dad," she protested, "Michael may not get here until seven or eight. We'd have to gulp down the soup and fish and race to the airport."

With amazing confidence, her father told her Michael would arrive much earlier than seven.

"And how could you possibly make that assumption about a man you met only yesterday?"

Nicholas had brought home a copy of the *San Francisco Examiner*, and he proceeded to open it up, making himself comfortable on the couch. "I'm a marvelous judge of character, Diana. He'll be clanging your cowbell soon."

"Have you added fortune-telling to your list of accomplishments?" she asked skeptically.

Her father didn't respond, and, as predicted, Michael was ringing the bell ten minutes later. Nicholas tactfully remained buried behind the newspaper to give Michael and Diana the privacy to greet each other properly.

Some of Diana's doubts melted away when Michael took her in his arms and kissed her. He looked at her as though she were a precious gift he had found under a Christmas tree. She attributed the guarded look in his eyes when he glanced over at her father to the inhibiting presence of a third party when he would have preferred to be alone with her.

She explained the change of plans. "My father has made reservations for a flight leaving at nine tonight. I offered to fix us something to eat here, but he insists on going out. If it's all right with you, we could drive him to the airport after dinner, in time for his flight."

Michael nodded in agreement. Flicking another glance at Nicholas, who had lowered the paper and was folding it neatly, he said, "If you're ready, Nick, we'd better get going."

Diana blinked. Nick?

While her father went to get his overnight bag, she glanced down at her suit. She hadn't had time to change, and was wearing the off-white suit and emerald-green silk blouse she'd had on all day. "I hope we aren't going anywhere fancy."

He scanned her outfit, a glow warming the dark depths in his eyes as he remembered the curves beneath the concealing fabric. "You'll do the way you are. The place I've chosen is informal." Then he added with a glint of mischief, "It's right up your alley."

The restaurant was called Doodles, and Michael was right. It definitely appealed to her. The walls were done in primary colors—red, yellow, and blue. Framed doodles signed by celebrities and large posters of crayons were scattered over the bright walls. Each table was covered with white paper, and a ceramic container of felt-tip pens, pencils, and crayons sat in the center.

After the initial shock of astonishment had worn off, Nicholas got into the spirit of the place. With a felt-tip pen he began to scribble on the table, clearly enjoying himself. He had expected some pomp, if not the circumstance, similar to the expensive restaurant where he had dined with Abe and Michael earlier. Now he realized Abe had been responsible for the choice of meeting place, not Michael. He was beginning to think Michael Dare was as remarkable a young man as he could wish for his daughter.

Diana, too, was happily drawing on the tablecloth. "How did you find this place, Michael? I've never heard of it before."

"One of the members of my research staff was talking about it. The minute she described the restaurant, I knew you would like it."

Pleasure soared through her. He had thought of her during his day at work. She liked that. "This place is wonderful. I love it."

Michael smiled when he saw what she was drawing. A line of ladybugs was marching across the table, with one veering away in the direction of the glass of water the waitress had set down in front of Diana.

He reached for a felt-tip pen and printed her name under the lone ladybug.

"Oh, thank you very much," she said with mock indignation. "You think I look like a ladybird?"

"It's ladybug, not a bird," he corrected her.

"If I'm going to have my name tagged on to an insect, I would rather it be a ladybird, as it's called in England. It sounds better than bug."

Under the cover of the tablecloth, he placed his hand on her thigh. "Ladybird it is."

His touch seared her leg through the fabric of her skirt. Ladybugs/birds, the restaurant, and her own father were all momentarily forgotten as she gazed into his smoldering eyes. A faint smile curved his lips, and his hand tightened briefly before he removed it.

The sound of her father clearing his throat brought her back to the reason they were at the restaurant. The waitress was waiting patiently to take their order. Diana felt her cheeks grow warm as her father raised a brow and smiled at her.

Nicholas kept the conversational ball rolling while

they ate. To Diana's astonishment, he regaled Michael with some of his experiences with reporters during the scandal eight years before. He talked frankly and with more amusement than bitterness, even when the tale wasn't remotely funny. That he was discussing that part of his life with a near-stranger was a revelation in itself.

Diana couldn't help but wonder why he was doing it.

Later they arrived at the large, busy San Francisco airport and found the departure gate with just enough time for Nicholas to hug her and shake Michael's hand. She assumed the "See you soon" was aimed at her, although he had been looking at Michael when he said it.

In the car, driving back toward the city, she said musingly, "Was it my imagination or was my father practically dancing toward that plane?"

"He did seem eager to get home. Maybe he misses your mother."

She shook her head. "It's more than that. It's as though a heavy weight has been lifted off his shoulders. I wonder what he and Abe are up to," she added as an afterthought.

Michael's head jerked around, his eyes sharp and searching. "Why do you think they're up to anything?"

"Just a feeling. I haven't seen him this carefree since before the scandal." She shrugged. "Well, whatever he and Abe are into, it's apparently good for my father."

Lord, he hated this secrecy, Michael thought. Thanks to Abe and her father, he was digging himself a hole he wasn't sure he was going to be able to get out of without its caving in on him. The fact that the two men had asked to be in his documentary wasn't going to make Diana any more receptive to the idea when she found out. And it was inevitable she would find out. She was already suspicious.

As they approached the exit that would take them to

his apartment, he asked, "What's your schedule tomorrow?"

"Another court appearance at one o'clock, then an English class at four."

He took the exit.

Diana glanced over at him but didn't say anything. Her bones were slowly turning to jelly. She was no longer frightened by the primitive restlessness in her body, the wanton desire she had to feel his hands on her body. She accepted it. She reveled in it. It was like learning a new language, a form of communication that used heightened senses instead of words. It was a language she had never been particularly interested in before she had met Michael. Now it was the most important form of communication she'd found.

As soon as his front door closed behind them, he reached for her. "I want you to stay here tonight. I'll take you home in the morning."

She didn't even pretend to think about it. "I'll stay."

"All night?"

"All night," she breathed softly, wondering why he felt he had to ask.

Without turning on any lights, he picked her up and carried her into his bedroom. The only light in the room came from the full moon, which shed its soft glow through the window. It was enough illumination for her to see the taut expression of naked longing on his face as he set her on her feet beside the bed.

Her suit jacket dropped to the floor as he eased it off her shoulders. One arm crushed her to him while his free hand began loosening the buttons on her silk blouse. "We'll talk in the morning," he said. "There's something I have to tell you." His hand parted her blouse, allowing him a glimpse of the delicate lace bra underneath. "But not now," he continued hoarsely, his breath quickening as the bra was swept away by his urgent hand. "Not now."

Diana made a whimpering sound and sagged against

him when he no longer supported her. With both hands he kneaded and caressed her tempting breasts. His eyes burned into hers as his thumbs rubbed roughly across the hard nipples, sending molten fire deep inside her.

Her hands trembled as she undid the buttons of his shirt and tangled her fingers in the curly hair covering his chest. Then she raised her arms to his shoulders and crushed her naked breasts against his chest.

With a groan he pushed her gently down onto his bed. He swiftly removed the rest of her clothing, then stripped off his own and lowered himself beside her.

"I wanted this to last all night, but I can't wait."

He saw the blue-green flames in her eyes and the soft, sensual smile on her lips as she lifted her arms in invitation.

Her arms enfolded him as he covered her arching body with his. A moan of pleasure escaped from her as he entered her at once, claiming her body as he had already claimed her heart. They were bound together by the silken threads of mutual need, entwined in the rhythmic act of possession. Fingers clenched and voices cried out when the summit of supreme satisfaction was reached.

Together they touched the stars before slowly drifting back to earth.

The moon's hazy light flowed over them as they fell into an exhausted sleep.

The sun was replacing the moon when Michael's hand stroked her satiny skin, from her hips, across her stomach, and up to the soft mound of a breast. He heard the change in her breathing and felt her immediate response, and knew she was awake.

Slowly her eyes opened and locked with his.

This time his lovemaking had a desperate quality, an urgency bordering on panic, as he took her. Reality would return with daylight, and he tried to ward it off with the magic he found in her arms.

After taking a shower, Michael leaned against the doorframe to the kitchen while he buttoned his shirt. Diana was making coffee. She was wearing his black robe, with the sleeves rolled up several times. The bottom of the robe was dragging on the floor. He could hear the soft sound of her voice as she hummed fragments of a tune while she puttered around in his kitchen.

He smiled. What a wonderful way to start a day. He liked having her here. Maybe too much. Too much to ruin it by telling her about the documentary just yet.

She nearly tripped over the robe on her way to the refrigerator. He stepped forward to steady her with his hand on her arm. "Careful. It's too beautiful a day for you to break your beautiful neck."

Hiking up the robe with her hands, she smiled at him. "That's a lot of beautifuls. For all you know it could be another foggy day."

He brushed a lock of tousled hair away from her face, a corner of his mouth curving up. "From where I'm standing, it's a beautiful day."

"You need a cup of coffee. You're raving." She opened the refrigerator door and shook her head at what she saw inside. "A mouse would have a hard time finding anything to eat in your kitchen, Michael. What do you usually eat for breakfast?"

"Coffee."

"That's all?"

He laughed at the horror in her voice. "I can see I leave a lot to be desired as a host. I'm not accustomed to having company in the morning either, goddess," he drawled, leaning down to kiss her briefly. "To make amends, I'll take you out for breakfast."

"Can I go like this?" she asked with a teasing smile, indicating the robe. "I don't have any clean clothes."

He poured a cup of coffee and handed it to her. "Sorry. The robe stays here. I'm the only man who ever gets to see you wearing it." Grinning, he added, "I could ask Mrs. Witherspoon to lend you something to wear."

"No, thanks."

The phone rang, and with a glance at his watch Michael went to answer it. Diana heard him order someone named Derek to get off his duff. Leaving him to sort out Derek, she returned to the bedroom.

After a shower, she put on the skirt and blouse she had worn the previous day. The blouse showed signs of having been tossed on the floor—which it had—and the skirt wasn't looking all that pristine either. She was studying her rumpled appearance in the mirror attached to the dresser when Michael spoke from the doorway.

"You should bring a change of clothes and leave them here so you won't have to look like an unmade bed in the morning."

Her eyes flew to his in the reflection of the mirror. For someone who implied he didn't have overnight guests, he was offering . . . what?

"I could," she said after a pause, returning her attention to her own image.

"But you won't."

Was that disappointment in his voice, or was she hearing what she wanted to hear?

She again met his eyes in the mirror. "No, I won't."

She took her comb from her purse and used it to gather her hair at the back of her head, winding it into a knot.

Michael walked toward her, raising his hand to stop her from securing her wadded-up hair with pins. "Leave it down."

With gentle but firm hands, he turned her around.

"Why does the thought of having some of your clothes in my apartment bother you? Do you like the idea of spontaneous one-night stands better?"

Anger flared in her eyes. "That's a terrible thing to say."

"I don't care much for it either."

"Then why say it?"

He heard the hurt blending with the anger in her voice, but he didn't let it distract him. "Because it needs to be said. I need to know our being together is more than a temporary episode in your well-traveled life. I would like some indication you are well and truly involved with me. Maybe a toothbrush and several items of clothing aren't exactly what I had in mind, but they would do for a start. I would like to see some piece of your clothing draped over a chair or hanging in the closet next to mine. Some tangible evidence that you were here and that you'll be back."

"It sounds like you want some kind of hostage—or would you call it a guarantee?"

"Am I asking for too much?"

Her uncertainty, her confusion, clouded her eyes, made her voice unsteady. "What are you saying? That you want a long-term commitment from me?"

His smile was fleeting. "Scares the hell out of you, doesn't it?"

"Don't be ridiculous," she said scoffingly. "Why would any type of commitment scare me?"

"I'm not sure, although I can make an educated guess."

She waited, not certain she wanted to hear what his guess might be. Crossing her arms defensively over her chest, she said, "Well?"

"You aren't used to having any stability in your life. You don't expect it. The only permanent fixtures are your parents and the Piccolos. I get the impression you don't like ties of any kind, and here I am asking for one."

It was as though a bulb had gone on, instantly imprinting every word he said in clear focus in her mind. She had never seen her life in the way he was describing. Was he right? Partly, she realized. She hadn't expected a permanent relationship with him.

She stood frozen in front of him, her eyes locked with his, her heart turning somersaults when it finally started beating again. She was tied to him more than he knew, tied and irreversibly bound to him.

After a long moment she turned toward the dresser, where she had placed her bag. She withdrew from it a slim rectangular object covered in a rich, dark leather. Releasing the catch, she opened it and set it on the dresser. Then she stood back and looked at him.

Michael stared at the object, then moved closer to examine it. It was a hinged frame containing two photographs. The picture on the left was a family portrait of Diana and her parents. The other showed a younger Diana standing next to a girl of her own age.

He looked at her. "You're willing to leave this here?"

"I don't have a toothbrush. This will have to do," she said with more lightness than she felt.

"Is the girl in the picture with you your friend Nicole?"

"Yes."

He carefully set the frame back on his dresser. "Do you carry this around with you all the time?"

She looked at him squarely. "Until now."

He drew in a long, painful breath. She had given him more than he had asked for, and he was overwhelmed. He was dazed by the extent of her generosity. As a token of her involvement with him, she was leaving behind part of herself, a symbol of the people she cared about most in this world.

Going to her, he took her in his arms and simply held her. There was no passion in his embrace, only tenderness and a deep feeling of gratitude.

"You won't regret committing yourself to me, Diana. I haven't given you any reason to believe me, but you'll have to take my word for it." A surge of possessiveness contracted the muscles in his arms. "It works both ways between us. I've never wanted to belong to any woman before, but I want you to know you have a claim on me too. You can lean on me, depend on me, and I'll always try to be there for you."

Her throat was tight with emotion. Her heart swelled with love. Before she started blubbering like a baby, she made an attempt to defuse her explosive feelings.

Raising her head, she asked, "Does that mean I can ask you for anything at any time?"

"Try me."

"If I ask you to feed me, you'll do it?"

Golden lights of amusement brightened his dark eyes. "That's how it works."

"Good. I'm starving."

Suddenly he laughed and gripped her waist to lift her up and twirl her around.

Her hands went to his shoulders, a great well of pleasure filling all the empty places she hadn't realized were inside her. So this was part of loving someone, receiving happiness while giving it. The responsibility for someone else's happiness was awesome, but the satisfaction was well worth any effort or sacrifice when it happened.

True to his word, he saw that she was fed. Then he drove her back to Sausalito. Their respective jobs demanded their attention until later, when Diana would meet Michael at his office after she was through with the English class.

The address Michael had given her was in a large high-rise building a block from the Trans Am Building. She rode up in the elevator to the eighth floor, glancing down at her gray houndstooth suit to make sure there wasn't any chalk dust on it. She straightened the collar of her cranberry silk blouse as the doors opened.

Several feet down the hall was an office with Michael Dare Productions painted on the frosted glass door. Pushing it open, Diana nearly collided with a tall bearded man whose arms were loaded down with folders and books.

"Tell me you're from Krager's," he blurted. "Put me out of my misery."

"Sorry."

A familiar masculine voice called from one of the interior offices, "Derek! Move it!"

Derek grinned sheepishly at Diana, who held the door open for him. "While I still have it, I'd better move it."

Laughing, she agreed with him. "Sounds like it."

The young man left, and Diana shut the door behind him. There was no one sitting at the desk in the outer office, so she headed toward the open door of the room Michael's voice had come from.

He was seated behind a cluttered desk, going over a stack of papers in front of him. When the phone rang, he lifted the receiver without looking up. He had a brief conversation with someone named Mandy about interior footage that needed to be reshot. He sounded resigned as he ordered her to go ahead and do it.

When he replaced the phone, he glanced up and saw Diana standing on the other side of his desk. The frown caused by the phone call disappeared instantly, replaced by a look of genuine delight.

He strode around the desk and reached for her. After he kissed her, he looked down at her and said, "Hi, goddess."

"Hi, tyrant."

"Tyrant? Where did that come from?"

"I literally ran into Derek, who was shaking in his boots for fear you were going to kill him."

He gave her an infectious grin. "Derek works better under fear of death. Otherwise he's content to sit around eating candy bars and reading science fiction books.

The only thing that keeps him off the unemployment line is the fact that he's one of the best cameramen around. He's in trouble because he misplaced some video tapes, so he's been scurrying around trying to find them."

There was the sound of something falling to the floor in the next room, followed by a woman's voice using a pithy foreign word. Then a petite dynamo dashed into the room.

"Michael," she said impatiently. "That idiot Andy just knocked my Rolodex off my desk. I need Krager's phone number to find out why they haven't delivered that tape."

"Krager's has the missing tape?"

"Derek called them this morning. They're supposed to send it over, but it's almost six o'clock and no tape."

Gesturing toward his desk he said, "Help yourself."

She spun the Rolodex file until she found the phone number she needed, then scribbled it down on a scrap of paper. Every movement was hurried but efficient, the woman's energy level high.

Before she left, Michael introduced her to Diana. "Carla, this is Diana Dragas. Diana, Carla Festino."

Extending her right hand, Diana told Carla she was pleased to meet her, speaking in Italian instead of English.

Carla's eyes widened, and she stood still, something Diana guessed she didn't do often. Replying in Italian, she asked, "How did you know I'm Italian?"

"You swore in Italian. It was a word not commonly found in any Berlitz class of conversational Italian."

Carla smiled. "You here for a job?"

"No," Diana answered simply.

Comprehension dawned on Carla's face. She nodded in Michael's direction. "You're the boss's girl. I bet you're the reason we haven't seen much of him lately." Carla gave her a measured look. "He's never brought a woman here before."

Diana glanced at Michael. "Never?" she asked Carla.

"Not that I know of. I've worked for him for over two years, and he's never let on he even had a personal life. I thought he was married to his work."

Before Diana could say anything else, Michael interrupted. "Hey, that's not fair. I keep getting these funny looks from you two and then you rattle away, knowing I can't understand a single word you're saying." Taking Diana's arm, he added, "Come on, I'll show you around."

She received a tour of the premises and met Andy, who was sorting through a stack of Rolodex cards in the office next door. There were two other rooms besides Michael's and Carla's. Diana was introduced to a couple of other staff members, a woman in her forties named Melba and another young man, this one with a bushy moustache. Both were getting ready to leave for the day.

All the offices showed evidence that this was a busy place. Folders, books, magazines, photographs, and storyboards, among other things, littered the desks and tables. Phones continued to ring even though it was past the normal closing hour. Computer cursors blinked on the terminals near several desks.

While Michael took care of a few last-minute instructions, Diana was corralled by Carla, who chatted with her in Italian until Michael was ready to leave. They said good-bye to Carla and drove to a nearby restaurant.

During the meal, they talked about a variety of things, movies they had seen, likes and dislikes, bits of their childhood.

Over coffee, Michael brought up the topic of Diana's ability with languages. "I've never seen Carla so animated. She usually just does her work with a minimum of conversation, but with you she talked a mile a minute."

"Italian is the language she's most comfortable with. She told me she still lives at home and both her parents prefer to speak Italian, especially her mother, who finds English very difficult to learn. People feel isolated when they have difficulty communicating. Some people can't learn a new language well enough to feel at ease when they speak it. They have to memorize the words and their meanings. A lot of people can't even manage that."

"I'm one of them. I tried to learn Spanish, but I kept getting the verbs in the wrong place."

"I've met people who could master another language but won't. Very intelligent people, who refuse to learn, even though they travel a great deal and do business with foreign companies. I've been an interpreter at meetings where there were three or four languages spoken and I was the only one who could understand what each one was trying to get across."

"Why didn't you work for the United Nations? I would have thought that would be a natural for you, after living in Washington."

"I find politics and diplomacy boring. Diplomats wrangle over the smallest detail, like whether a comma or a semicolon is needed in a document. It's more interesting to free-lance."

She told him about several incidents where she had been in the middle as translator, peacemaker, and referee. That led Michael to an anecdote involving an English film director who kept telling the actors on a movie lot in Hollywood to stand on the pavement. They stood in the street, but he wanted them on the sidewalk. As Diana already knew, a pavement in England is called a sidewalk in the States.

She wanted to hear more about Michael's work. Seeing him at his office had been enlightening. She had been exposed to another side of the multi-faceted man she loved, and she wanted to learn even more.

When she asked him point-blank what he was working on at present, she didn't get a direct answer. The office had been bustling with activity, so there was definitely some project underway, but he wouldn't talk about it.

"Are you superstitious?" she asked.

He blinked in surprise. "I don't walk under ladders, but I call that good sense, not superstition. Why do you ask?"

"I thought perhaps you considered it bad luck to discuss what you were working on. Nicole won't let anyone see her paintings until she's completely finished. Says it's bad luck."

Michael grabbed at the excuse she had furnished. "I would rather you wait and see the program when it's finished."

"I don't have a television set, remember?"

"I have several. We'll watch it together." He switched the topic of conversation to his past work. "Since you have an in with the director, I'll show you the documentary on homeless people. I have it on tape in my apartment. That is, if you want to see it."

Her eyes sparkled. "I'd love to. I'll even bring the marshmallows."

They watched the documentary that night. When it was over, Michael gently dried her tears, accepted her lavish compliments, and began to make love to her on the carpet in his living room while the credits crawled across the screen.

The next day, Friday, he flew to Los Angeles on business, but said he would be back on Saturday morning and promised to spend the weekend with her.

This time he didn't ask her to go with him.

When he returned on Saturday, he seemed preoccupied, and there was a desperate quality to his lovemaking that left Diana puzzled. Several times he seemed to be about to tell her something, but didn't.

Within a few hours, though, he was the Michael she knew. Throughout the weekend he was attentive, possessive, and loving. They were together every moment, thoroughly wrapped up in their cocoon of companionship and lovemaking.

Until Sunday night.

Michael announced he had to return to Los Angeles and would be gone all week. He had been unusually tense and withdrawn the entire evening, and only when he made love to her did the Michael she knew and loved return to her. He was breathtakingly passionate, with an intensity that drove every other thought out of her head.

Afterward, she nestled against him, staring into the darkness while he slept.

Nine

Michael was gone when Diana woke on Monday morning, but he phoned her that evening. He sounded strange, as though it were an effort just to say hello.

She settled her pillow against the headboard of her bed and leaned back against it. "Have a rough day?"

"So-so. How was yours?"

"It was fairly normal. Nothing exciting."

The hard, weary edge in his voice softened. "No more shoes thrown in courtrooms?"

"Not a one. How about you? Have you killed Derek yet?"

His deep chuckle vibrated over the phone lines. "He's alive and well and was happily munching away on a candy bar when I saw him about an hour ago."

She heard him take a deep breath of relaxation. "You sound beat."

"I was before I called you. You're good for me, goddess. I would rather be there with you, but the sound of your voice will get me through the night. What were you doing when I called?"

"Just a second, and I'll show you." She pushed the "play" button on the cassette machine beside her and held the receiver close to it. After a few sentences she switched it off, then spoke into the receiver. "Are you still there?"

"I'm still here." He sounded amused. "You're either

entertaining a Japanese gentleman or you're learning Japanese."

"I'm *trying* to learn Japanese."

"It figures." He changed the subject abruptly. "What are you wearing?"

"What?"

"What are you wearing? I want to picture you in my mind exactly as you are right now." When she didn't reply right away, he pressed her for an answer. "Diana, I'm not asking for the theory of relativity. It's a fairly simple question. Tell me what you are wearing."

"Ah . . . a T-shirt."

"And?"

"That's it."

"I had to ask." The sound he made was part growl, part groan. "Well, go put some other clothes on."

She laughed. "Why? You can't see me anyway."

"I have an active imagination where you're concerned, goddess, and it's working overtime at the moment." He paused, and added, "Damn, I wish I were there with you. This is turning out to be a long week."

"It's only Monday."

"I know. There are four more long days to get through. Oh, hell. Go back to your Japanese gentleman. I'm going to take a cold shower and sulk. Good night, goddess. I hope you sleep better than I will."

"Good night, Michael," she said softly.

It was late the following night when Michael called again. He didn't say much about his work other than it was going as well as could be expected. He asked about her day and once more wanted to know what she was wearing, then said he missed her like hell.

"It feels like I've been cut in two with a dull blade."

There was an involuntary catch in her voice when she admitted, "I've gotten to the point of calling airlines to check on flights to Los Angeles."

A few seconds went by. Then he said, "As much as I would love to see you, don't fly down here. I wouldn't have much free time to spend with you. I want to wrap up the inter—the taping this week. One of the sponsors will be in town, and I'll have to entertain him sometime too. I just don't have any spare time right now."

A simple "stay put" would have sufficed, she thought. She had been only half-serious, but he'd made it clear her coming to Los Angeles wasn't one of her better ideas. It might not rate high as ideas went, but she felt he was explaining too much, giving her reasons that sounded more like excuses.

"It was just a thought I had at a weak moment," she said. "I have a lot of work to do myself, so I couldn't come anyway. In fact, I'd better get to some of it right now."

Michael detected the change in her voice. "Diana, it isn't—"

"If you're too busy to phone me tomorrow night, I'll understand."

"Diana."

"Good night, Michael."

The following day Diana kept thinking about the phone call from Michael, unable to pin down the reason for the disturbing intuition nudging her, telling her something was not quite right.

She could understand his dedication to his work, but she couldn't understand the secrecy surrounding it. He didn't want her to know whatever it was he was doing, and that bothered her. She was positive he had been about to say he wanted to wrap up an *interview*, until he switched it to say *taping*. She hadn't a clue why he had changed what he had been going to say. So he was going to do an interview. That was part of what he did for his documentaries. She didn't understand why he was trying to conceal the fact.

It was a part of his life he was keeping from her, an important part. Granted, she had initially shown a distaste for journalism, but after seeing it, she had praised his documentary on homeless people. There should be no doubt in his mind of how much she had approved of the show and his sensitive handling of the plight of homeless men and women. She had been moved to tears, full of compliments, and honest in her reactions.

Even if she had never seen a sample of his work, she wouldn't have allowed her prejudice to color her opinion of his upcoming documentary. She knew Michael better now. She knew whatever he did would be done with sensitivity, honesty, and would be factual.

Somehow she was going to have to convince him she had changed her viewpoint about journalists, at least his kind of journalism. She still abhorred the reporters out for a sensational headline no matter who they hurt in the process, but then, Michael held the same opinion about reporters digging for dirt. She wanted him to feel he could share his work with her. It was up to her to convince him she respected that work.

She was late getting home that day. The session in court translating for Mr. Burkhardt had lasted longer than it should have, thanks to the German's hot temper flaring up at the slightest provocation. Tact and diplomacy had been needed as she translated each outburst, leaving out the less-than-complimentary curse words, as she'd told Mr. Burkhardt she'd do. His lawyer had finally warned Mr. Burkhardt that he was going to lose the case for himself if he didn't shut the hell up.

There had been only one other minor eruption after the warning, when the owner of the car dealership was on the stand, denying every allegation. Justice had prevailed, and Mr. Burkhardt had been awarded a financial settlement. The triumphant German had insisted on taking his lawyer and Diana out to celebrate.

It had turned out to be quite a party, including Mr.

Burkhardt's wife and two sons and their families. Diana had to rush to catch the last ferry of the day, which left at eight o'clock, arriving in Sausalito at eight-thirty. Usually she looked forward to the long walk home, but tonight she had taken a taxi. It had been a long day, and she had been too tired to walk home.

She hoisted the pennant as usual as soon as she arrived home, even though she couldn't see any light on over at the Piccolos'. Whenever they came home, they would see the pennant and know she was there.

She changed out of her business suit, tugging on a pair of snug cut-off jeans and a T-shirt, leaving her hair loose on her shoulders. After fixing herself a sandwich, she sat down at the kitchen table to correct a test from the English class. After a few minutes, she pushed her chair back and walked over to the stereo to put on a record. It was too quiet. The raspy, distinctive voice of Rod Stewart filled the room, and she returned to the table.

When the phone rang an hour later, she got up to answer it, thinking it might be Michael. But Nicole was on the other end of the line, and she wasn't calling just to chat. She was concerned about her parents.

"I phoned them several times last night and again a few minutes ago. There's no answer. I was hoping you'd know where they are."

"I haven't seen them for several days, but I'm sure they're all right, Nikki."

Nicole wasn't pacified. "It's not like them to go away for any length of time without letting me know where they'll be. I thought maybe they'd told you."

Diana could hear the concern in Nicole's voice. "I'll check with some of the other neighbors. Someone may know where they've gone. They may have flown down to Palm Springs to see my parents." She didn't think it was very likely, since her father had just been in Sausalito, but he and Abe might have made some plans to get together while her father was visiting.

Nicole didn't buy that. "But they always tell you if they're going on a trip, so you can water Mother's plants and keep an eye on the houseboat."

"Well . . . ah, I haven't been home all that much, and when I am, I haven't been alone."

There was a long pause, then Nicole asked quietly, "So that's still on, is it?"

"As far as I know." Changing the subject, Diana asked a question of her own. "Is there any particular reason you need to talk to your folks? Are you all right, Nikki?"

"Lord, I hate that question. Yes, I'm fine."

"I thought maybe you were trying to contact your parents because you were—"

"I'm fine," Nicole repeated. "I've been so busy painting for the show in November, I haven't had time to write to my parents, and I know how they worry about me, so I decided to call. Now it's my turn to be worried about them."

"I'll phone my folks and talk to the neighbors, and I'll call you back as soon as I find out anything."

It was going on ten o'clock when Diana phoned Nicole. "I'm sorry, Nikki, but no one around here seems to know where your folks are. I called my parents, but no one answers there either. The four of them have probably gone off on some tour or other. They've done that before."

"They've always let us know where they are going. It's not like any of them just to disappear without telling us anything."

Diana remembered how secretive her father had been during his recent visit, and she had the feeling Abe and her father had cooked up some trip or something when they were together.

"All we can do is wait and see if we get a postcard or phone call from them."

"I suppose so," Nicole said. "It's so odd that they would just take off like that, though. You don't suppose they're up to something they shouldn't be doing, do you?"

Chuckling, Diana asked, "Like what?"

"Remember the time in London they went to the Savoy Hotel for a formal dinner and on the way home stopped at a carnival to ride on the carrousel in full evening dress?"

Diana smiled, wishing she could have seen her ever-so-proper mother hiking up her long dress to sit side-saddle on one of the carrousel horses. Promising to call if she discovered where their parents were, she eventually hung up and returned to correcting the English tests.

The wall clock in the living room had just finished chiming eleven times when she heard the bell by the front door clang. She jumped up from the table and rushed to the door, expecting to see Rena or Abe or both of them. She stared in shock after opening the door, when the porch light shone on the man standing there.

"You're in Los Angeles."

Michael's only reaction to her dim-witted remark was a slow smile. There were lines of fatigue around his eyes and mouth, and he was leaning against the doorframe as if he needed its support to keep him upright. One hand was tucked into the pocket of his jeans, and the other held a tan jacket over his shoulder by one finger. His white shirt was open at the neck and slightly rumpled.

In a voice hoarse with exhaustion he asked, "Can I come in?"

She took a step backward to allow him to enter, and he pushed himself away from the doorframe and into the room. He tossed his jacket onto a chair and reached for her. He held her tightly against his body, as though he were a drowning man and she his lifeline.

"Oh, Lord, I missed you," he murmured against her ear.

"I thought you were so blasted busy."

Michael felt the stiffness in her body and heard the coolness in her voice. It was the same tone he had detected on the phone the night before, prompting him to make a flying trip there.

"I had to see you or go out of my mind," he said.

Her doubts and uncertainties evaporated. Whatever his reasons were for keeping his work separate from his relationshp with her didn't matter as long as he was with her. It was when he was gone that her overactive imagination took over, conjuring demons.

She lifted her hands to stroke his face, her fingers rasping against his unshaven skin, bringing his mouth down to hers.

She fed the hunger deep inside him and arched her body into his to feast on the delicious sensations caused by the intimate contact. She felt him sway against her, and concern overrode her desire.

"Michael, you're exhausted."

He buried his face in her neck, his arms keeping her slender form locked to his hard body. "I haven't slept too well the last couple of nights."

That was obvious. "When do you have to be back in Los Angeles?"

"I told the pilot ot meet me at the airport at seven in the morning. Lord, you feel good in my arms."

"You chartered a plane?" she asked in astonishment.

"Hmm," he murmured against her throat. "It was the only way I could get here tonight and be back in L.A. by nine tomorrow morning."

Diana was speechless. It was a full minute before she could take in the fact that he had chartered a plane in order to spend a few hours with her.

When she felt his body tremble against hers, a vast wave of protectiveness overcame her. He was practically dead on his feet. She drew away from him to take his hand and lead him to her bed.

"Where are we going?"

"You're going to bed. You can hardly stand up."

"Only if you're going to bed too. I'm not going to spend another night hugging a damn pillow."

She gently pushed him down so he was sitting on the edge of the mattress, then knelt to remove his shoes. He cooperated fully, helping her undress him, until he noticed she was still fully dressed. Using the last of his strength, he removed her clothing. He pulled the covers back and lay his head on the pillow, bringing her down with him.

When she was tucked into his side with her head resting on his shoulder, he sighed heavily and closed his eyes. His arms held her securely and didn't ease their hold even when he fell into a deep sleep.

Diana remained awake for a while, giving herself time to get over the shock of having Michael beside her when she had expected to have to spend another lonely night without him. She wasn't disappointed that he had fallen asleep immediately without making love to her. It was enough he had traveled so far just to be with her, just to hold her, just to be near her.

Remembering his comment about needing to be at the airport at seven, she eased out of his arms long enough to set her alarm for six. A frown appeared on his face, and he was suddenly restless when she left his side. The frown disappeared as soon as she snuggled against him, once again in his arms.

A lone thought gave her confidence in their relationship and made her smile as she drifted into a dreamless sleep.

Michael had a deep need to be with her, to be near her, even for only a few hours. He hadn't flown from Los Angeles for the sole purpose of making love to her, but to see her and hold her.

The shrill ringing of the alarm roused them from a sound sleep.

Michael lay on his side with his arm over her rib cage, as she lay on her back. "What the hell is that?" he mumbled.

"The alarm clock."

"Throw your shoe at it."

"You may have noticed I don't happen to be wearing any shoes." She flung her arm over and shut off the alarm.

Still with his eyes closed, he moved his hand over her rib cage and down her stomach to her thigh. "You don't appear to have *anything* on."

His warm hands caressing her flesh aroused her, reminding her of other times, of dark nights of passion. Using the philosphy that what's good for the goose is good for the gander, she rolled onto her side and allowed her hands to journey over his firm waist and hips.

"Hmm. You don't have anything on either. Fancy that."

She felt his immediate response hard against her stomach and heard him suddenly catch his breath when her slender fingers closed around him.

His moan of pleasure was lost as he rolled her onto her back and plunged his tongue into the sweet recesses of her mouth. The coil of desire tightened almost painfully between them as their need expanded with each intimate kiss, each urgent stroke and caress.

The coil snapped. Michael covered her body with his and parted her legs. Lifting her hips to meet him, he thrust into her satin heat. Her body clenched around him, and he lost what little control he had started with.

The days and nights apart had sharpened their desire to a fine line between a primitive ache and a demanding urgency. They surrendered to the sweet agony, plunging into the rhythm of lustful passion, clinging to each other as they fell into an exploding chasm.

Six alarms could have gone off in his ear and Michael

would have let them ring. He didn't want to move. For the first time in days, he felt complete and at peace. There was no longer any doubt in his mind about the cause. She was lying in his arms.

The clock on the bedside table was ticking away the precious minutes. Finally he pushed away from her.

"I don't want to, but I have to go."

"I know." She sighed. She watched him as he threw back the covers and reached for his clothes.

When he was fully dressed, he sat on the edge of the bed near her hip. His forefinger stroked her soft cheek. "You're a special lady, Diana. Do you know that?"

Her hand closed around his wrist. "You make me feel special."

He leaned down to kiss her. "I'll try to get back on Friday night. If not, I'll see you on Saturday morning. We need to talk, but there isn't time now. It will have to wait until this weekend. Okay?"

Her hand dropped to her side. She didn't want him to leave, but she couldn't ask him to stay. "Okay. Would you like some coffee?"

He shook his head. "I don't have time." He smiled. "I'll have plenty of time this weekend. Ask me again then."

"You got it," she murmured as lightly as she could, ignoring the tightness in her throat. She pulled the sheet around her and started to slide her legs over the side of the bed.

He placed his hand on her shoulder to stop her. "Stay in bed. I'd like to think of you still lying here while I'm flying back to L.A."

He kissed her again and got to his feet, then looked down at the lovely picture she made, with her tousled dark hair spread out on the crisp white pillow. This vision would have to last him the rest of the week.

With one last look he left her, quietly closing the front door behind him.

Diana rolled onto her side and hugged the pillow he

had used, closing her eyes as she absorbed his scent lingering on the pillowcase. With a soft sigh of contentment, she fell into a light doze.

The insistent ringing of the phone woke her, breaking into a wonderful dream, in which she and Michael were walking along a beach at sunset.

She got out of bed and grabbed her robe out of the closet on her way to answer the phone. She glanced at the clock on the wall in the living room. It was five minutes after eight.

"Hello?"

"Diana? It's Nicole. I know where our parents are."

Sitting down on the chair beside the phone, Diana asked, "Where are they?"

"In Los Angeles. Mother called me this morning."

A prickly premonition stabbed her. "What are they doing there?"

Nicole didn't like to be the one to tell Diana, but someone had to do it. "Your father and mine are taping interviews for Michael Dare's documentary. The program is about people who were once in the public eye but have retired or faded in popularity. It's to be called, 'Where Are They Now?' "

The color drained from Diana's face. She wanted to believe Nicole had misunderstood her mother, but deep down inside she knew it was the truth.

Too many incidents fell into place, now that she knew about the interviews. Her father's unexpected arrival, the lunch with Abe in the city and her father's cheerful mood afterward, Michael's reluctance to discuss his next documentary.

"Diana, are you still there?"

Rousing herself from her tormenting thoughts, she said, "I'm still here. I was trying to make some kind of sense out of the whole thing. Why all the secrecy? Why didn't they tell us before they left?"

"Well," Nicole began awkwardly, "they all know how you feel about the media, Diana, especially when your family is involved. Your father is telling his side of the story involving the Russian diplomat. They know how touchy you are about publicity, so they didn't say anything to you."

"I see," she said in a wooden voice. "I didn't realize I was such a threat. Why are you telling me about this program now if I'm not supposed to know about it?"

"My mother overheard my father telling your father about his interview yesterday with Michael Dare. She got the impression your father's tape session is today. Mother thought you should know."

Which was why Michael had to be back in Los Angeles that morning, Diana thought. "I can't believe your mother didn't know about the program."

"Neither did your mother," Nicole said. There was a hint of humor in her voice as she added, "From the indignant tone of my mother's voice on the phone, I gathered they're making the three men's lives miserable."

"Three men? Who's the third man?"

"Michael Dare. Who else? If your mother could have found him last night, she would have made mincemeat out of him. She found out from your father that Michael was seeing you and hadn't told you about the documentary either."

Her mother hadn't found Michael because he had been in Sausalito in her daughter's bed.

"He was here," she said in an unemotional voice. "He left early this morning."

Nicole sighed. "I'm sorry, Diana. If it's any consolation, he's in for the rough edge of your mother's tongue. She's already torn strips off your father's hide. To be fair to Michael, it sounds as though he was caught in the middle."

"He should have told me what he was doing. My father too. I wouldn't have objected or tried to stop them. I might not have approved, but if he wants to appear on television to tell his life story, that's his decision, not mine."

"Who knows how men think? I certainly don't. What-ever their reasons were for all the secrecy, the cat's out of the bag now. Give me a call if you need someone to talk to, or come up to the mountains if you feel like getting away for a while."

"Thanks, Nikki. Right now I need to think this through and decide what to do."

"I understand. Keep in touch."

"I will. Thanks for calling."

After hanging up the phone, Diana remained in the chair for a long time. Her mind was a grab bag of mixed emotions. She could reach in and pull out an-ger, disappointment, hurt, doubt, and love, but she wasn't ready to examine any of them yet. She was feeling too raw and vulnerable just then to make any rational decision or come to any major conclusions.

What bothered her more than anything else was that Michael hadn't trusted her enough to tell her what he was doing, even when it concerned her own father. She had to admit that part of the blame for his feeling that way fell on her. She had been extremely vocal about her opinion of journalists when she had first met Michael. Apparently she hadn't made her new feelings, her broader viewpoint regarding journalists and their work, clear to either him or her father.

It was ironic that she was actively involved in help-ing people communicate, by teaching languages and translating for people who needed to disseminate infor-mation in a foreign tongue. Teacher, teach thyself to communicate.

The chiming of the clock reminded her of the pass-ing time and appointments to keep.

She made it through the day with few problems. After the English class at the rec center, Antonio stayed in the room once the others had left. Usually he was one of the first to dash to the door and freedom.

"Is there something you wanted, Antonio?"

"Sì, I mean, yez." He had gotten that far, but was

unable to go any further. His tough act disappeared, and he was struggling with whatever it was he wanted to tell her. Instead of looking tough, he looked like what he was, a fifteen-year-old boy with a problem.

Breaking her own rule about only speaking English in the classroom, Diana spoke in Italian. "Tell me in Italian, Antonio. I can't help if I don't know what your problem is."

It all came out in a flood. His mother had received some medicine from a doctor, along with a sheet of instructions. They were written in English, and no one in the family could understand all of it. He didn't know anyone else to ask. Would she translate the instructions for his mother? He had the paper with him, but Diana wouldn't take the chance that Antonio might get something wrong once he was home.

He escorted her to his home, an apartment four flights up in an old Victorian building. The minute the door was opened, a cacophony of sounds hit Diana. Four children were sprawled on the floor and sofa, watching cartoons on television. The three girls and small boy were chattering away in Italian, in competition with the TV characters.

Antonio's mother was in her early forties but looked fifty. Worry and illness had taken their toll on her Neapolitan beauty. She welcomed Diana to her humble home once Antonio had introduced her and explained why she was there.

The instruction sheet was presented along with a cup of cappuccino, and Diana sat at the large dining-room table to write out the instructions in Italian. She was horrified to discover how important they turned out to be. Mrs. Cortesini was a diabetic, and the instructions were the strict diet she was supposed to follow.

Diana went through the diet carefully with Antonio's mother to make sure she understood how important it was. The doctor had explained the insulin dosage, so that was no problem, but his nurse had only handed Mrs. Cortesini the diet sheet, without giving her any explanation.

Mr. Cortesini arrived home from work shortly after Diana had gone over the diet for the third time. His younger children threw themselves at the burly man, who opened his arms to engulf each and every one of them. Antonio's hair was mussed by his huge hand by way of a greeting.

In a booming voice Mr. Cortesini invited Diana to stay for dinner. The table groaned under the abundant bowls of spaghetti, sauce, and bread, but it was considerably lighter by the end of the meal.

When it was time for Diana to leave, Mr. Cortesini insisted on driving her home, and Antonio wanted to ride along. He hoisted her up into the cab of an old pickup truck. A blanket covered the torn seat. She asked Mr. Cortesini what he did for a living, and he told her he delivered vegetables to grocery stores. He was saving money so he could have a small grocery store of his own someday. The family had moved to San Francisco only six months before, to be near his brother and his family.

When they arrived at Gate Five in Sausalito, Antonio accompanied Diana to her houseboat. When he saw where she lived, she went up several notches in his opinion.

She thanked him for walking with her to her door, and reminded him, "It's back to English in class, Antonio."

"English is hard to learn."

"It will get easier. Good night, Antonio."

He grinned and said in English, "Good night, Miz Dragas. Thank you for help."

"You're welcome. See you in class."

He nodded and walked back to the truck.

Inside, Diana turned on several lights and kicked off her shoes. She was about to hoist her pennant outside when the red blinking light on her answering machine caught her attention. She played back her messages.

There was only one.

"Diana, this is Michael. I need to talk to you. Please call me." He quickly gave a number in L.A. "No matter what time you get home, call me. I won't be asleep."

She looked at her watch. Though he had said he wouldn't be asleep no matter when she called, she didn't immediately go to the phone.

First she changed into her robe and let down her hair, brushing it out to fall in a heavy mass on her shoulders. They she filled the teakettle with water and set it on the stove to heat. Using her mother's remedy for just about anything, she measured tea leaves into a brown teapot and set out a cup and saucer. The familiar activity was automatic, giving her time to think about Michael and what she would say to him.

When the tea had steeped, she poured a little milk in the cup and added the fragrant tea and a teaspoon of sugar. As she stirred her tea, she walked over to the wide window in the living area and stared out at the dark bay.

Like the tea, her thoughts had steeped during the day. She could separate what was important and what wasn't. Her relationship with Michael was important. Her wounded pride wasn't. If her father wanted vindication in the form of an interview on Michael's documentary, it was entirely his decision and had nothing to do with her. That was between him and his mother.

If she was going to have the kind of relationship she wanted with Michael, the conflict over her work had to be resolved. That was between her and Michael.

She drained the cup, and set it down on a table. Then she walked over to the phone and punched out the number Michael had given her.

Ten

The phone rang three times before it was answered by a sleepy feminine voice. "Hello?"

Thinking she must have the wrong number, Diana asked, "Is this room 326?"

The woman's reply was a muffled, "Yes."

"I would like to talk to Michael Dare."

"He's not here."

Diana was in the process of slamming down the phone when she heard the other woman shout her name. She brought the phone back to her ear. "Diana, don't hang up. It's Carla."

"Carla?"

"Yes. I'm sorry I'm so foggy. I fell asleep."

"Michael left this number for me to call. Is he there?"

"No. He told me to wait in his room in case you called. I'm supposed to find out what your schedule is tomorrow."

"Where is Michael?"

"I don't know. It's been crazy around here. The wives of the two men he's been taping are causing an unholy ruckus. Oops! I forgot. One of them is your mother. I think he's gone somewhere with your mother."

Diana couldn't help feeling a little sorry for Michael. Her mother could be quite intimidating when her English dander was up. "Tell him I returned his call, Carla."

"Sure, but wait. I have to get your schedule for Friday."

"Why?"

"Because he told me to get it from you."

It was no use questioning Carla any longer. She was only following orders, and didn't seem to know what was going on either. "I'll be home after three in the afternoon."

"Got it. I'll tell him."

Diana hung up the phone and poured herself another cup of tea to drown her disappointment. She had been ready to talk to Michael, and now she was going to have to wait.

She might as well go to bed and try to get some sleep. Tomorrow might prove to be a very interesting day.

While Diana was getting ready for bed, Michael was leaving the Dragas suite, in the same hotel where he had a room. He returned to his room and shook Carla awake.

"Carla, wake up. Did Diana call?"

Rubbing her eyes as she sat up, Carla said drowsily, "Yes." She squinted at her watch and muttered, "About thirty minutes ago."

"How did she sound?"

Carla blinked. "What?"

"Did she sound angry, or what?"

Looking at him warily Carla replied, "She sounded normal, I guess."

"Did you find out when she'll be home tomorrow?"

"You mean today. It's after midnight." She saw his scowl of impatience and gave him the information he asked for, without further delay. "She said she'll be home after three."

"Okay. Thanks, Carla. Come on, I'll take you to your room, so you can get some sleep."

A few minutes later he was back in his own room to shower and change clothes. Dressed casually in jeans and a navy sweater, he slipped on his jacket and put an assortment of keys in his pocket after checking to be sure he had them all. There was one for his room, one for the rental car, and several for the film studio. Next stop was to get a thermos of coffee from the hotel kitchen.

It was going to be a long night.

Diana was home by three o'clock, but she didn't stay there. At around four, Rena phoned to say they were back and to ask her to come over right away. Diana promised to be over as soon as she'd changed her clothes. Even though she was curious to hear what had happened in Los Angeles, she took the time to shower and slip into white slacks and a silk blouse the same shade of turquoise as her eyes. She brushed her hair and tied it at the nape of her neck with a white ribbon.

A glass of Chablis was shoved into her hand as soon as Rena opened the door for her. She was escorted into the living room, where Abe was seated in one of the comfortable, upholstered chairs, a glass of wine on the table beside him.

Sitting on one end of the couch, Diana looked from Abe to Rena.

"Are you the advance guard, to check out the temper of the opposition?" she asked, and smiled as Rena and Abe exchanged startled glances.

Rena relaxed a little when she saw Diana's smile. "We weren't sure how you would take the news about the interviews. I phoned Nicole as soon as we arrived home, and she said she had called you and you knew what was going on in Los Angeles." She paused for a moment. "You don't seem very upset."

Diana sipped her wine before answering. "Why should I be upset? It's got nothing to do with me." Shifting her gaze to Abe she asked, "'How did the interviews go?"

"Very well. I was quite pleased." He gave her a puzzled look. "I don't understand your attitude, Diana. Your father and I thought you would disapprove of our participation in Michael's documentary. Lord knows, Rena and your mother did. We went to a great deal of trouble to prevent you from learning about it." He slanted a quick glance in his wife's direction. "We ended up in a lot of trouble because we didn't tell anyone, and you sit there as cool as you please."

Diana grinned. "I could throw a temper tantrum if it would make you feel better, but I'm not angry. I'm sorry you all felt I would be a pain in the neck about the whole thing, though. You based your decision on my reaction to journalists eight years ago, didn't you?" He nodded. "I'm not sixteen now, and Michael is not one of those sleazy reporters who hung around us like mongrel dogs, hoping to get a juicy tidbit thrown their way."

Abe leaned back in his chair. "Well, I'll be damned."

"You will be if you ever do something like this again without telling me," Rena said emphatically.

Diana took another sip from her wineglass. "Which is exactly what I'm going to say to Mr. Michael Dare when I see him."

The sound of a heavy pounding on the front door made all of them jump in surprise. Rena recovered first and got to her feet. "You may have your chance sooner than you thought, Diana."

Whoever it was beat on the door again; then Diana heard Rena open the door and say, "She's in there."

Michael appeared in the doorway almost immediately, pausing there for a second until his searching gaze found her on the couch. Along with looking thoroughly exhausted, he gave the impression of someone who was determined about what he was doing.

In several long strides he crossed the room to her. He casually said hello to Abe over his shoulder as he reached down for Diana's arm. He tugged her to her feet, then congenially said, "Good-bye, Abe," as he marched Diana toward the door.

Rena's eyes widened in surprise as they passed her, and she replied absently to Michael's polite good night.

Diana went willingly with Michael, without a single protest, until he turned her in the opposite direction from her houseboat.

"Where are we going?"

"To my apartment."

"Why? My place is much closer."

"You don't have a television set."

Her mouth fell open. After all that had been going on during the last couple of days, he wanted to watch television?

"Michael, I don't want to watch television. We need to talk."

They had reached his car, and he opened her door. But instead of insisting she get inside, he clamped his hands down on her shoulders. "Diana," he said roughly. "I've been awake all night. I've been raked over the coals by an expert; namely, your mother. I'm tired, I'm hungry, and I'm in a rotten mood, so could you just this once button up?"

"Will I get a chance to speak eventually?"

"Yes."

"I'm buttoned."

"Good."

The trip to Michael's apartment was silent. Michael finally spoke after they'd entered his apartment and he had closed and locked the door behind them.

"Sit down on the couch, facing the television screen."

Knowing he had carefully scripted how the evening was going to proceed, Diana did as she was told.

He turned on the set and pushed a couple of buttons on an oblong machine next to the television. Then he came over to the couch, carrying a remote-control gadget, and sat down beside her.

A few seconds of blurred snow on the screen were replaced by a clear image of her father sitting in a Queen Anne chair in a living-room setting. He looked relaxed and completely at ease as he talked to a person not in the picture. That person was Michael. He asked her father what he was doing now that he was no longer working as a diplomat, and Nicholas briefly mentioned his involvement in real estate and golf.

Eventually the topic of the scandal eight years before was brought out in the open, giving Nicholas an opportunity to tell how an innocent friendship with a young diplomat had been distorted by the press. He described how careers had been ruined and friendships tested, with few passing the test, while many failed.

The tone of the interview was neither bitter nor apologetic. Her father responded to Michael's prompting with straightforward facts, presenting them with honesty and in the proper sequence.

The interview lasted nine minutes, and when it was over Michael used the remote control to rewind the tape. Then he handed the control to Diana.

"What am I supposed to do with this?" she asked.

He pointed to one of the buttons. "If you don't want the interview to be included in the documentary, press this button. This tape is the only copy."

The button had the word *erase* printed on it. The magnitude of his offer stunned her. By the simple action of pressing a button, she could wipe out her father's chance to exonerate himself, to set the record straight once and for all.

Michael's gaze shifted from the control device to her face. "I've told your parents what I was going to do with the tape. They have agreed to let you decide whether or not it will be included in the documentary."

"I don't want that kind of responsibility. The choice
s my father's, not mine." She shoved the control back
into his hand. "Here. I don't want this thing."

Getting to her feet, she began to pace the floor. "I
on't believe this. I just bloody don't believe this. Ev-
ryone has gone right round the twist. My father goes
o unbelievable lengths to make arrangements to ap-
ear on your program without telling me or Mother,
s if it's a state secret. Then . . ." She placed her
ands on her hips and faced Michael. "*Then* he
grees to let *me* destroy the tape? Why would he do
uch a thing?"

"Because he loves you."

Michael's quiet statement deflated her indignant pos-
ure. She sank down onto the couch. "What does his
oving me have to do with whether or not he appears
n your program?"

Michael shifted sideways on the couch and stretched
is arm out across the back, his hand only a few
nches from her head. "Your father knows how painful
he scandal was for you and your mother. He was
rying to protect both of you, but at the same time he
eeded to tell what really happened eight years ago. He
as going to present the interview to you and your
nother after it had been done, hoping you would ap-
rove. If you didn't approve, the interview wouldn't be
ncluded in the documentary."

"Why were *you* going to allow me to erase the tape?"

"Because I love you."

She stared at him, afraid she hadn't heard him cor-
ectly. "Wh—what did you say?"

For the first time that afternoon, he smiled. "Is it
eally so hard for you to believe? I love you, Diana
Dragas." His fingers wove gently through her hair. "If
our father's appearance on my show upsets you, then
t won't be shown. Your happiness is more important
o me than your father's interview."

With his other hand he held the remote-control de
vice out to her. "*You* are important to me, Diana. If yo
don't want the interview to be in the documentary
erase it. It's my way of proving to you that you are mor
important than having your father's interview."

She took the remote control and tossed it onto th
coffee table. "Screw the damn documentary. I'm sick o
hearing about it." Her eyes never left his face. "Do yo
really love me?"

He laughed and reached for her, pulling her ove
onto his lap. "There isn't another woman like you
goddess. I figured that out when I saw you throw
shoe at that kid with a gun in my uncle's courtroom
You haven't done one single thing since then to mak
me change my mind." His arms tightened around he
as though he wanted to imprint her body onto his
"Yes, I love you. You make me come alive in a way tha
causes me to wonder how I ever thought I was conten
with my life before I met you."

Her arms slipped around his neck, bringing her hea
closer to his, her lips almost touching his. "*S'agap
poli.*"

It was difficult for him to concentrate with her mout
so close to his. "What does that mean?"

Her stunning eyes glowed as she looked up at him
"It's Greek. It means I love you very much."

His dark eyes held hers for a long moment, findin
her vow of love reflected in her eyes. He kissed he
gently, tenderly, until her lips parted under his. Th
strain of the past week was forgotten. Only the relie
and exultation remained, blending with the wonder o
learning she loved him.

The weight of his body pressed her down onto th
cushions, his mouth possessing hers with unconcealed
love. He took her love and gave his back to her. Ever
though he had all the time in the world, he couldn'
wait any longer to lay an elemental claim to her. The

ad said the words, and now he wanted to feel them,
 be so close to her, to belong to her as she would
 him.

He shifted his body off hers temporarily, keeping one
g over hers as he unbuttoned her blouse. She smiled,
 soft, sensual invitation. He parted her blouse and
wered his head to taste first one breast, then the
ther, hearing the soft sounds she made deep in her
roat as his tongue rasped over her tender flesh.

He brought his mouth up to hers again. Against her
ps he murmured, "I was afraid I'd never be able to
uch you again. I never want to feel that way as long
s I live."

Her hands stroked down the corded muscles of his
ack. "As long as I live, you won't have to feel that
ay."

His mouth opened over hers as his hands began to
emove her clothing. His breathing grew ragged with
eed.

Diana removed his shirt, and her nails raked over
is chest, lingering on the hard nipples.

Her tantalizing touch was his undoing. Within sec-
nds he had stripped off the rest of her clothing and
rn off his own. He met her arching hips with his,
sing himself in her velvet heat with powerful strokes.

She closed her eyes to savor the heady pleasure he
as giving her. She was drowning as sensation after
ensation flowed through her, and she didn't want to
e saved.

Their passion accelerated until the rush of satisfac-
on was found, and they touched the stars, then held
ach other tightly during the trip back to earth.

When Michael finally was able to move, he eased his
eight off her and lifted her into his arms. In his
edroom, he laid her on the bed. He shoved his alarm
lock in the drawer of the bedside table and unplugged
e phone. Satisfied that he had covered any chance of

an interruption, he lay down beside her and pulled her
into his arms.

Diana had watched him with lazy amusement. "You
forgot the quarantine sign for the front door."

"If I had one, I would put it out. I want you all to
myself, with no interruptions."

"Until when?"

"Until forever," he muttered sleepily. "Or tomorrow
morning, if you have to get technical."

She could feel his body relax, and realized his many
hours without sleep were catching up with him. Her
own eyelids were becoming heavy. Knowing there would
be a lot of tomorrows for them released the inner coil of
tensions that had built up over the past week, and she
too, fell asleep.

Because they had gone to sleep early, they woke early
and showered together. Afterward Diana slipped on
Michael's robe and made coffee while he shaved.

When the coffee was finished Diana poured two cups
and was about to take Michael's to him when he entered the kitchen. He took the mug from her and told
her to bring hers into the living room.

"Why?"

He brushed a brief kiss across her lips. "There's
another tape I want you to see."

She groaned. "Not another one?"

His hand pressed against her back to guide her toward
the couch. "Yup. 'Fraid so. I was going to show you
this one last night, but somewhere along the way I
got sidetracked."

She sat down and drank from her mug of steaming
coffee while he exchanged tape cassettes and stabbed a
couple of buttons before sitting beside her.

Diana almost dropped her coffee cup when she saw
Michael's face on the screen. She jerked her head around
to look at him. "What is this?"

"Watch and find out."

She watched. The Michael on the screen began to talk to her.

"According to a relative of yours, a wise woman who knows you well, I have made a colossal error in judgment by not telling you about the interview I did with your father. It is small comfort to know your mother said exactly the same thing to your father, substituting herself as the injured party."

Diana chanced another glance in Michael's direction, but he pointed toward the screen.

"Your mother made it clear there must be honesty and communication in marriage, along with love, if the marriage is going to succeed. I thought she was discussing her own marriage, but she said she was talking about marriage in general. Since I want to stay on your mother's good side, I plan to take her advice. Also because she is right."

The Michael on the screen had Diana's complete attention now. She set her coffee cup on the table and leaned her elbows on her knees.

"I promise always to tell you the truth, in the present and the future. If you serve me a tuna casserole with those little crushed potato chips on top, I will suggest we eat out that night. If you want six children and I only want two, we'll compromise and have four. We'll compromise, we'll discuss, we'll debate. Whatever it takes. According to your mother, that's how it works. I will share my home, my income, my faults, my name, and my love with you for the rest of my life."

The camera came in for a close-up. "I am asking you to be my wife, my love, the mother of my children, and my friend. If the answer is yes, please say so to the man next to you. If the answer is no, please reconsider."

The screen went blank.

She slowly turned to the man next to her. "I want to hear one part over again."

He obliged. "I love you. Will you marry me?"

She flung herself into his arms, toppling him onto his back. "Yes."

It was his turn for clarification. "Yes, what?"

"Yes, I love you." She kissed him. "Yes, I'll marry you." She kissed him again, this time more leisurely. His arms came around her, holding her on top of him.

Her voice was husky with emotion when she spoke. "I'll be your friend, your lover, the mother of your children. What else was there?"

"My wife."

"And your wife, forever and longer."

THE EDITOR'S CORNER

Seven is supposed to be a lucky number . . . so look for luck next month as you plunge into the four delightful LOVESWEPT romances and the second trilogy of the Delaney series. Has the Free Sampler of **THE DELANEYS OF KILLAROO** made you eager to read the full books? (Whenever we do a book sampler I get the most wonderful letters of protest! Many of them very funny.) As you know from the creative promotion we've done with Clairol® to help them launch their new product, PAZAZZ® SHEER COLORWASH will be available next month when the Delaney books, too, are out. Think how much fun it would be to do your own personal make-over in the style of one of the heroines of **THE DELANEYS OF KILLAROO**! *Adelaide, The Enchantress* by Kay Hooper has hair like *Sheer Fire*; *Matilda, The Adventuress* by Iris Johansen has tresses with the spicy allure of *Sheer Cinnamon*; *Sydney, The Temptress* by Fayrene Preston has a mystery about her echoed in the depths of her *Sheer Plum* hair color. Enjoy this big three!

And for your four LOVESWEPTS, you start with **A DREAM TO CLING TO**, LOVESWEPT #206. Sally Goldenbaum makes her debut here as a solo author— you'll remember Sally has teamed up in the past with Adrienne Staff—and has created a love story that is filled with tenderness and humor and great passion. Brittany Winters is a generous, spirited woman who believes life should be taken seriously. This belief immediately puts her at odds with the roguishly handsome Sam Lawrence, originator of "Creative Games." Sam is a wanderer, a chaser of dreams . . .

(continued)

and a man who is utterly irresistible. (What woman could resist a man who calls her at dawn and tells her to watch the sunrise while he whispers words of love to her?) **A DREAM TO CLING TO** is an enchanting book that we think you will remember for a long time.

PLAYING HARD TO GET, LOVESWEPT #207, is one of Barbara Boswell's most intriguing stories yet. Slade Ramsey is the proverbial nice guy, but, jilted by his fiancee, he got tired of finishing last. Figuring women really did prefer scoundrels, he tried hard to become one. However, he was only playing the part of a charming heartbreaker, and he never got over the love he felt for the first woman he had treated badly—young and innocent Shavonne Brady. When he comes face to face with Shavonne, gazing again into her big brown eyes and seeing the woman she has become, Slade knows he can never leave her again. But how can he convince her that the man she knew a few years ago—the one who had broken her heart—isn't the real Slade? Barbara has written a truly memorable story, and not only will you fall in love with Shavonne and Slade, but all of their brothers and sisters are unforgettable characters as well.

In **KATIE'S HERO** by Kathleen Creighton, LOVE-SWEPT #208, Katherine Taylor Winslow comes face to face with Hollywood's last swashbuckling star, Cole Grayson. Katie is a writer who always falls in love with the heroes of her novels. Now she's doing a biography of Cole . . . and he's the epitome of a hero. How can she fail to fall for him? Katie and her hero are as funny and warmhearted a pair as you're ever likely to find in a romance, and we think you are going to be as amused by Katie as a tenderfoot on Cole's ranch as

(continued)

you are beguiled by the tenderness of a hero who's all man. This book is a real treat!

Only Sara Orwig could turn a shipwreck into a romantic meeting, and she does just that in **VISIONS OF JASMINE**, LOVESWEPT #209. After the ship she and her fellow researchers were on sinks, Jasmine Kirby becomes separated from her friends, alone in her own lifeboat. She is thrilled when she is rescued, but a little dubious about the rescuer—a scruffy sailor with a hunk's body and a glint in his eye that warns her to watch out for her virtue. Matthew Rome is bewitched by Jasmine, and begins to teach her how to kick up her heels and live recklessly. When they meet again in Texas, Jasmine is astounded to discover that the man she'd thought was a charming ne'er do well actually lives a secret and dangerous life.

Four great LOVESWEPTs and three great Delaney Dynasty novels ... a big Lucky Seven just for you next month.

With every good wish,

Sincerely,

Carolyn Nichols

Carolyn Nichols
  Editor
LOVESWEPT
Bantam Books, Inc.
666 Fifth Avenue
New York, NY 10103

It's a little like being Loveswept

SHEER MADNESS

SHEER COLOR

SHEER PASSION

SHEER EXCITEMENT

SHEER INTRIGUE

SHEER ROMANCE

All it takes is a little imagination and more Pazazz.®

Coming this July from Clairol...Pazazz Sheer Color Wash —8 inspiring sheer washes of color that last up to 4 shampoos.

Look for the Free Loveswept *THE DELANEYS OF KILLAROO* book sampler this July in participating stores carrying Pazazz Sheer Color Wash.

NEW!
Handsome Book Covers Specially Designed To Fit Loveswept Books

Our new French Calf Vinyl book covers come in a set of three great colors—royal blue, scarlet red and kachina green.

Each 7" × 9½" book cover has two deep vertical pockets, a handy sewn-in bookmark, and is soil and scratch resistant.

To order your set, use the form below.

LOVESWEPT

Love Stories you'll never forget by authors you'll always remember